For my mother, Joann. Without her, this book would not have been possible. The gentle support and encouragement she freely gave me throughout my life gave me the courage to believe in myself to achieve my dreams. I know that her star in heaven shines brighter than all the rest.

Gina VanSicklen

... AND THE STARS SMILED

AUSTIN MACAULEY PUBLISHERS™
LONDON • CAMBRIDGE • NEW YORK • SHARJAH

Ordering Information
Quantity sales: Special discounts are available on quantity purchases by corporations, associations, and others. For details, contact the publisher at the address below.

Publisher's Cataloging-in-Publication data
VanSicklen, Gina
… And the Stars Smiled

ISBN 9781647503956 (Paperback)
ISBN 9781649790941 (Hardback)
ISBN 9781649790958 (ePub e-book)

Library of Congress Control Number: 2021916690

www.austinmacauley.com/us

First Published (2021)
Austin Macauley Publishers LLC
40 Wall Street, 33rd Floor, Suite 3302
New York, NY 10005
USA

mail-usa@austinmacauley.com
+1 (646) 5125767

O na hoku no na kiu o ka lani

"The stars are the eyes of heaven."

The stars secretly observe all.

They're looking for the good that's within us and that surrounds us and how we can do the same, every minute of each day.

Hawaiian saying

Prologue

The mourners gathered around the grave listening to the pastor say his final words. The warmth of the autumn sun couldn't penetrate the haze of sorrow that smothered the group. The sound of stifled sobs broke through in fractured bursts. Everyone stood in silence not wanting to leave until one brave soul started the procession. The hugs, handshakes and solemn nods were endless. The last two people stood side by side staring at the flower-covered casket. The crushing pain of their loss made it hard to breathe. They interlocked their arms and slowly made their way to the waiting car. The ground beneath them held them in place and they turned to face each other and joined hands. One of them spoke with a shaky voice,

"Please promise me that one day you will…"

Chapter 1

June, 1981

Sunny was getting ready for THE party of the school year. She was belting out, You're My Best Friend along with the radio that sat on top of the white and gold claw footed dresser. She applied her makeup not letting the butterflies in her stomach make her hand shake. She took her time, it had to be perfect. Pleased with the outcome, Sunny skipped across the purple shag carpet to get dressed. The new outfit purchased for this special night, was flattering in all the right places. Sunny glanced up her poster of Peter Frampton covering the flowery wallpaper she was starting to outgrow. "Sorry, Peter, tonight's the night. I am going all the way with Teddy tonight." She giggled.

As she brushed her long golden-brown hair her thoughts wandered to Teddy and she wondered what his face would look like when she told him she was ready. Sunny planned their life out. They would marry after college, live in their hometown and have three children. Her best friend Kate would live on the same block with her husband. The thought of living anywhere else never entered her mind. She loved her little town on the south shore of Long Island; some of her best childhood memories were rooted here, like walking down Main Street, where the shop owners knew all of the neighborhood children, just saying hello to everyone she met. It was where she belonged. Seaville was part of who Sunny was, it was home.

Chapter 2

Sunny threw her hairbrush on her canopy bed as her mom entered her room. Joann looked at her daughter with a smile on her kind face.

"Sunny, you look adorable. My little girl, sweet sixteen and never been kissed," Joann said.

"Not for much longer, Mom," Sunny said with a chuckle.

"Which one, being kissed or being sixteen?"

"It's both, Mom. My birthday is coming soon and I'm probably going to kiss Teddy tonight!"

They embraced and laughed. Sunny was glad that her mother couldn't read her mind because if Joann Marino found out what Sunshine had planned she would lock her in her room for the next sixteen years.

Joann's smile faded when she thought about Teddy kissing her daughter. It was subtle and Sunny didn't notice. Joann was not a fan of Teddy. His charming smile and smooth talking always came off as condescending and arrogant to her. Joann didn't welcome him with the open heart that her daughter did. There was something about him that Joann felt was not trustworthy. She had never expressed her feelings to her daughter because Sunny was so smitten with him, but she never let her guard down around him either.

Teddy arrived at Sunny's house right on time. He came to the door and flashed his dazzling smile to Joann who returned her usual polite smile and nod. The teens bid her mother goodbye, jumped into the green Buick and were on their way to the party.

Sunny turned to Teddy and said, "I still can't believe your parents bought this car for you. It is so cool."

Teddy shrugged, "They were so happy that I signed scholarship papers to Adelphi University. Now they don't have to worry paying about tuition. They said they earned this scholarship too after all of the track meets they had to sit through over the years." Teddy was their youngest son and they loved to indulge him.

Sunny sat right next to Teddy so he could put his arm around her as they cruised. He would always lean in and steal a kiss at red lights. Oh, how she loved those red lights and snuggling so close to him. As they drove to the party Sunny went back to daydreaming of their life together. She pictured an old Victorian house with a big front porch overlooking lush, colorful gardens and the most magnificent, fragrant lilac bush there ever was. Sunny loved lilacs. She would go to her grandma's in the spring when her lilacs bloomed. Her grandma's bushes were tremendous and she would have to use a ladder to reach the best blooms. Sunny brought home big bouquets and put them all over the house. No matter where she stood in her house she could smell their enticing scent. She always kept the biggest bouquet for her room. Sunny could just picture their three children riding bikes with their friends and all piling into

Sunny's kitchen for snacks that she lovingly prepared for them. Teddy would be the perfect husband going off to work every day in the suits she had cleaned and pressed for him. He's so handsome. His job in the city would be enough so that Sunny could stay home with the children. When the children were old enough, Sunny would start her career as a nurse. Yes, she had their life together figured out. She believed she knew exactly where her life was going; she had no idea that the night's events would change everything.

The party was in full swing by the time Teddy and Sunny arrived. The chatter was loud, the music louder and the atmosphere was charged with excitement. Sunny's bones vibrated to the beat of the music. Tonight would be awesome. She was trembling with anticipation.

As they made their way to the back yard, the girls' field hockey team were signing each other's jerseys as they walked past. They squeezed past a group of people standing around the keg and made their way further into the yard to where the whole track team was chanting Teddy's name as they approached. She was proud to be on his arm.

Sunny kept her eyes scanning the crowd for Kate, her best friend. The two had been friends since nursery school. The families became friends and the two girls, inseparable. Kate and Sunny loved each other like sisters.

Sunny tugged on Teddy's arm when she spotted Kate, Teddy put his arms around Sunny's waist and she tilted her head up to meet his eyes. Teddy kissed her, the kind of kiss that was soft, tender and filled with teenaged love. It left her breathless and reaffirmed her decision to go all the way with him tonight.

"Go talk to Kate, I'm gonna hang with the guys."

Sunny responded with a kiss to his cheek and caught up with Kate. The girls wandered about the party alternating chatting and giggling, catching up on their day. Kate just knew her friend was busting to tell her something.

Kate looked at her friend and said, "Spill it, Sunshine Rey."

Batting her eyelashes she said, "What would you like me to spill, Clara Katherine?" They usually refrained from using their given names in public but Kate had started it.

"What are you hiding? I know you and you are not telling me something, so I will say it again, SPILL IT."

"You know me so well, tonight is the night, I am going to go all the way with Teddy," she whispered the last part.

Kate grabbed Sunny by the arms as her eyes widened. "Sunny, are you sure?"

"I am. I feel ready for this."

Kate let out the breath she didn't know she was holding. "I want all the details tomorrow. Well maybe not all. But you have to tell me what it's like so when I meet my Mr. Wonderful I know."

Sunny promised to give her a full report and they hugged and squealed with delight.

The girls danced, laughed and mingled around the party until Sunny realized that she hadn't seen Teddy for a while. Usually when they went out, throughout the night their eyes would lock and she would blow him a kiss or Teddy would mouth, "I love you." It always made her belly flutter. She turned to Kate and asked, "Have you seen Teddy?"

"No," Kate replied.

The girls started looking around the party for Teddy. At first they were casually glancing around for him as they wandered through the backyard, but when they realized they hadn't seen the track team either, that's when Sunny became apprehensive. A strange feeling was bubbling deep inside her, something was not right. Until now, she thought it was her plans causing this feeling but right now she was sure that was not it. She checked the patio where people were dancing, a seating area where someone was talking and everyone around him was laughing, the pool was set back without a person nearby and just past the pool was a shed. Everyone but Sunny was having a good time at that moment. Kate was beside her and elbowed Sunny as she motioned toward the shed. Sunny shrugged and headed toward it. As she approached her heart began to race and she thought it might beat right out of her throat. If he was drinking tonight of all nights she would be really pissed off. The feeling started to turn to worry. She would have to get him home somehow and he would have to explain why his car wasn't home. Being drunk would ruin everything tonight, how could he? Stupid.

See, you finally decide to go all the way and look what he does. Maybe you should wait. Her face started to flush. As she approached the shed she heard voices, they were chanting Teddy's name and she stopped dead in her tracks. She became furious.

She turned to Kate, "He's probably chugging a stupid beer."

They turned the corner of the shed and the group came into view. Sunny was looking from person to person absorbing the scene and at that moment she wished he was chugging a beer.

There was Teddy standing in the center of all his buddies with Corinne, the school dirty girl and skank extraordinaire, rising from her knees. It took Sunny a minute to process everything and when she did, she saw red. Everything began to unfold in slow motion in front of her, she could hear Teddy curse, she saw his friends scurry away and Corinne, in her haste to get away nearly knocked Kate over. Kate quietly walked out of ear shot to give the couple some privacy.

Sunny looked squarely at Teddy. "What the hell do you think you are doing?"

"Nothing, what are you so freaked out about?" He had a smirk on his face.

"Are you kidding me?"

Teddy shrugged gave her one of his looks that would usually make her knees weak. But right now it just made her want to punch him in his handsome face.

"I was looking all over the party for you, worried that you might be drunk. Instead, what do I find? These assholes are cheering while that dirty skank is doing God knows what to you. Really? With Corinne? You make me want to throw up. How could you be so horrible?"

Sunny felt like someone was inside her head trying to break out with a hammer. She had never been so angry in her life. Teddy actually looked amused, which infuriated her even more.

With the same arrogant smirk on his face, Teddy looked into her eyes, "You don't need to get so upset, I am going home with you." Sunny started to say something but his words continued. "Corrine was just for fun; it was a dare.

There is no reason for you to be this worked up. I am your guy."

He leaned in to embrace her and give her one of those kisses that used to leave her breathless. Sunny almost let him get close enough to do just that when she put both hands up and placed them on his chest to push him away.

"Stop!"

The smile fell from Teddy's face, "What? No kiss?"

"That's right, no hug, no kiss until I have an explanation of what happened."

She was seeing a side of Teddy that had never reared its ugly head before. This was not her Teddy. How could he be so callous? If he loved her why would he think of doing anything with anyone else? She couldn't even entertain that type of thought. This boy standing here, that she thought she loved, turned into someone she didn't know.

Teddy tried to brush it off. He told her it was nothing and she should stop worrying about it. She was stunned. They stood there staring at one another for what seemed like hours. As she looked at Teddy, the life she planned for them flashed through her mind and she realized that he didn't have the same dream. He didn't love her the way she loved him. Maybe he thought he loved her. But she deserved to be loved the way she wanted to be loved with respect and tenderness. It was in that moment she knew it was over for her. There was nothing he could say that would make this okay and she was not going to get past it.

Sunny thought she would feel all kinds of emotions. But in her heart instead of sorrow, anger, fear or sadness she felt okay. She was calm and sensed that everything was as is should be. No drama, no make-up, no boyfriend. Done. She had the incredible feeling that this just worked out for the best. She surprised herself. She felt weird. Sunny thought she should be crying right now, but the tears didn't come. The feeling was so much more intense than that but she had no idea how to put it into words. Weird was the word she kept coming back to.

She smiled, looked at Teddy's handsome face, "You're right I am going to stop worrying. In fact, I won't concern myself with this for another minute."

She gazed into his eyes. "Goodbye, Teddy. Have a nice life."

She turned slowly around and walked away from him. He started to go after her and then thought to himself that he would give her some time to cool off.

"I'll see you tomorrow," he called out, but she kept walking.

Chapter 3

When Sunny emerged from behind the shed Kate ran toward Sunny firing questions off like crazy. The questions were coming faster than Sunny could process them.

"Was that Corinne?

Did you fight?

Was Teddy drinking?

Is he still back there?

Oh my God what was Corinne doing?"

Sunny took her arm and sat in the pool area. The pool was quiet and they could be alone. Sunny needed a few minutes to gather her thoughts and answer Kate's questions. Sunny explained everything to her friend, who listened patiently. Kate had her arm draped around Sunny's shoulders squeezing and releasing with love as she told her everything. Sunny rested her head on her friends' shoulder as they sat by the edge of the pool. They dangled their toes in the water. She knew that she could rely on this girl holding her. They sat in silence for the next few minutes. They laid back and stared up at the cool dark night sky. It was their favorite kind of sky, no moon, dark, crystal clear and the stars looked like you could reach out and grab one. It was a like a Fire Island night sky, the best of all. Kate wanted to get Sunny home but Sunny wasn't ready yet. Kate pointed out a cluster of stars to Sunny, sat for a few more minutes with her friend and then asked her if she wanted some time to herself. Sunny just nodded.

Kate reluctantly started to get up; she looked to her and asked if she was sure, Sunny gave her a half smile and nodded to reassure her she would be fine.

"I just need to gaze by myself for a few minutes." Kate headed back to the crowd to chat and pass the time until she could take her friend home.

Sunny knew if she went home now her mom would be asking all about her night and why Teddy did not bring her home and she just wasn't ready for the inquisition. She decided to stay at the pools' edge and dangle her feet in the cool water for a while. She was leaning back on her hands and let her head drop back to gaze at the night sky. The stars brought her such a sense of peace. She could feel the weight of the evenings' events pass through her. The perfectly planned life was gone, her perfect boyfriend was not so perfect and the beautiful family she dreamt of was gone. She couldn't believe that she was about to give her virginity to him this same night. She felt like an idiot. Now what? She needed time to herself, time to be Sunny again. Perhaps she could stare at the stars and let them tell her what to do. She let out a breath and closed her eyes to everything and everyone. This felt better. The chatter and the music from the party faded into the distance. It felt good to just be in the moment and let her feet skim the water as her mind cleared.

Sunny sat like this for a while, head hanging back, feet dangling, eyes closed, sensing the stars watching her and drinking in the night air. The stillness of the night began to change. The air had an aura of electricity; she imagined that the stars were sending little pulses that danced on her skin. The hair on the back of her neck stood up, in a good, goose bumpy kind of way. She sensed a presence. When she opened her eyes to look around at last, standing near her was a boy, one she never heard walk up to her. At first glance she knew this boy was unfamiliar. A better look told her that he was not a boy but a man. He was older than she was, maybe nineteen or so. He looked at her with an intensity that penetrated her soul. Sunny was captivated by him. She couldn't look away and she didn't want to.

His face was strong, kind of squared and his eyes twinkled like stars. They were the most beautiful green, Caribbean Sea green, like the water from the cruise she went on with Kate's family last winter.

His chin had a dimple that looked delicious. Sunny thought of filling it with peanut butter and kissing it. Her thoughts were firing off in every direction like the electrical pulses she felt. His lips above that dimple looked perfectly kissable and the corners of his mouth were curving up slightly. His smile was dancing on the edge of becoming full blown.

Oh my God I have lost my mind, how could I react to a stranger like this, what is wrong with me? Word of the night…weird.

Sunny held his gaze, her eyes were locked the stranger. His eyes were locked on Sunny as well. As she was mesmerized by him he was transfixed on her.

She squeaked out a barely audible *Hi.*

The stranger unleashed his smile and it was all she imagined and more. His eyes twinkled even more as the smile danced its way up to them. Her heart started to beat faster just looking at him and the butterflies that once belonged to Teddy now belonged to Mr. Ocean Eyes.

"Hi, yourself. Mind if I sit?" his voice reminded her of the caramel sauce she poured over ice cream sundaes at Sprinkles every summer.

"Sure," she uttered huskily.

They sat side by side in silence. They felt the charge between them. It felt like a thunderstorm rolling in off the ocean. But it was a clear, still night. Sunny and Mr. Ocean Eyes sat without speaking for a while, processing the sensations. Sunny was surprised by these vibes. Was it because the insanity of the night? She was going over all of this in her head when the silence was broken by Mr. Ocean Eyes.

"Perfect night for star gazing."

Sunny wondered if he was kidding. Kate must have sent him out here to make sure I was okay. She told him to talk to me about stars! She was too much and the best friend ever.

She gave him a smart-ass look which he returned and said, "What?"

"How do you know Kate?"

"Who?" said Peanut Butter Dimple.

He genuinely did not know what she was talking about. Sunny thought she could feel his answer, like they had a connection, that weirdness again. She let it go and agreed that it was a perfect night for star gazing. They sat and looked up at the sky side by side.

"Sorry I thought you knew…never mind," Sunny said to the star gazing stranger.

"I'm Jack." He extended his hand to Sunny.

As she took his hand in hers, a thrilling shiver radiated through her hand and right up her arm.

"I'm S – Sunny."

"Nice to meet you, S – Sunny. Are you at the party alone?"

"No, I am with my friend, Kate; she's around here somewhere."

"No boyfriend here with you?" Sunny bumped into him when he was standing by the keg and he was sure she was with a boyfriend.

"Nope."

Jack tried to disguise his happiness and asked her about school and Kate. Time flew by and it was time for her to go, Kate must be worried. She stood.

"Well, Jack, it was nice to meet you."

"The feeling is mutual S – Sunny." He stood and placed a hand on her shoulder. It was back, that crazy ripple of electricity that made her want to throw her arms around him. Their eyes locked.

"May I call you?"

Sunny answered with a smile as bright as a full moon. She wrote her phone number on his hand with a pen he handed her and she wondered where he kept it.

He looked at his hand satisfied with the outcome, leaned in and kissed her on the cheek. Her knees felt like Jell-O. She hoped they would hold her up. She was speechless as she watched him walk away with his hand open so the ink wouldn't smudge.

She floated off to find Kate. After Teddy's betrayal tonight she expected to be mad, sad, hurt or anything but excited. She was really excited. Sunny's instinct was to run as fast as she could to find Kate and tell her everything. In that moment Teddy was forgotten. Sunny was trying to comprehend her encounter with Jack. Brief but intense? Connected? She wasn't sure how to describe it or what she could call it, the only thing she knew for sure is that she wanted more.

Kate and Sunny found each other and left the party. They decided to walk home. Sunny wanted to tell Kate all about Jack but she didn't have the words yet. Sunny needed a little bit of time to process all that she felt. Kate told her she saw someone with her at the pool and Sunny tried to sound casual.

"Yeah that was Jack he just sat with me for a bit. He seemed nice." Sunny decided to keep Jack to herself for the moment.

The girls talked all the way back to Sunny's house. Sunny asked Kate to stay the night and she agreed. As they approached the house they spotted the green Buick parked out front. The girls exchanged looks.

Kate said, "I'll go inside and let your mom know we are home."

"Thanks, I'll be in soon."

Teddy got out of the car and approached Sunny with a contrite look on his face. He professed his remorse and asked Sunny to forgive him.

"I love you, Sunny. Corinne was just a stupid prank, a dare. She didn't mean anything to me at all. You're my girl, Sunny. You know how the guys are, babe."

He kept talking about how what he'd done was no big deal. After ten minutes of Teddy justifying what he did, she held up her hand and cried, "Enough!"

"Please stop talking."

She had a sad, half smile on her face as she looked at Teddy. He read her look as a sign of her forgiveness. What he failed to notice was that her smile stopped at her mouth. It didn't spread across her face and it didn't even come close to her golden-flecked brown eyes. He leaned in to embrace her mumbling how glad he was that she understood. Sunny placed her hands on his taut chest, looked into his handsome face and pushed him away.

She held his gaze. "I understand, Teddy. Now you need to understand too. Tonight I was going to make love with you, tonight I felt ready to make that commitment with you."

He was dumbfounded. "Really?"

"Right now I am thanking my lucky stars that I didn't. I was so happy to be your girlfriend. In my dreams I saw this wonderful life we would have together. In your arms I felt safe and loved."

"Babe, you are, you know that." He reached for her again and her words stopped him.

"I thought I did, I believed in us. What you did tonight ripped that dream into pieces. If I let you put your arms around me now I would betray myself. It is not okay, Teddy."

"I'm sorry, Sunshine, I'll make it up to you."

"You can't, it is done. I deserve someone who loves all of me with all of him. I was so hurt when I saw you behind the shed with Corinne. I am not even sure exactly what went on but in my heart of hearts I know it was betrayal. I know I would never treat you like that."

In that moment, looking at Teddy, Sunny believed that he was really sorry. But his actions broke them in two.

"You need to go home now, Teddy, we are over."

Teddy looked surprised and asked, "Were you really going to make love to me tonight? Why didn't you tell me?"

"Would it have made a difference?" Sunny asked. "I would have done anything for you, I thought I really loved you."

"Thought you loved me huh?" Teddy said as he shrugged his shoulders. "If it means anything to you now, I truly am sorry. I still love you, Sunny."

"I know you believe that, Teddy, and for what it's worth I'm sorry too." And she turned and started walking toward her house.

Sunny stopped and turned back toward Teddy. She ran to him and hugged him hard before placing a gentle kiss on his lips and whispering goodbye.

Chapter 4

Sunny's mom was in the kitchen and Kate went upstairs already. Her mom hesitated a minute because she knew something was up.

"Teddy and I broke up; it is done for good."

Joann hoped that the happiness she felt didn't shine through.

"I will tell you all about it tomorrow, Kate's staying over tonight. Okay?"

"Of course, Lovey, I'll call Florence and let her know."

Sunny kissed her mother and ran upstairs to Kate. Sunny and Kate spent the weekend together and Kate was there when Jack called. Sunny nearly knocked Kate down running for the phone when her mom called her.

"Hi, Jack." Sunny tried to sound calm. But she was a bundle of nervous energy.

"Hello, Sunshine, how are you today?"

"Great, I was just hanging out with Kate."

"Would you like me to call another time?"

"No, Kate will be fine, this is her second home, in fact, she may be in the shower or something." Sunny scrunched her face at the words exploding from her mouth. She took a deep, calming breath.

"Cool, what are you guys doing today?"

Jack wanted to climb through the phone and hug Sunny. He was trying to get the nerve to ask her out on a real date but ended up talking about yard work. This didn't go the way he planned. He needed a new plan.

Sunny was on the phone with Jack for a long time but Kate didn't mind. Sunny's face lit up as she spoke about him. Kate felt the excitement radiate off Sunny. She liked being a part of it. Kate couldn't believe that Sunny had let go of Teddy so easily, not that she blamed her, what he did was so stupid and she would have felt the same way. Clearly Teddy and Sunny were not meant to be. But Jack on the other hand…maybe he was the one.

Kate stayed over on Sunday night too. Usually their moms would not have allowed a school night sleep over. But Sunny's mom thought she needed her friend after the breakup, so she talked to Kate's mom and they agreed. The girls laid in bed listening to their favorite radio show, Psychic Sundays. They fell asleep listening to stories from the other side.

Sunny and Kate walked into school together on Monday morning knowing everyone would be talking about the *breakup*. The cliques whispered to each other as Sunny walked by. She did her best to concentrate on her classes and ignore everything else going on around her. When the afternoon bell rang, Sunny felt a wave of relief wash over her and headed out the back door of the school. That's when she saw him.

Jack was leaning against a Camaro, her favorite type of car. She couldn't decide which was more gorgeous Jack or the car. And just like that the crazy thoughts started firing off in her head again. Kiss his lips. Hold him tight. When Jack saw her, his smile slowly spread across his face. He was even more beautiful in the sunlight. He wins. She made her way over to him trying to catch her breath.

"Hi," she said.

"Hi yourself," Jack responded.

"What are you doing here?"

"I came to pick up my sister."

Sunny felt a pang of disappointment, he was not here to see her.

"Does your sister go to school here?"

"Yep, Hannah is a freshman, involved in every club she could join and she is the best little sister anyone could ever want."

Sunny loved the way he talked about Hannah with love and pride. She was fascinated by this, being an only child herself. She envied sibling relationships sometimes and clearly Jack was an awesome brother. Sunny was ready to give in to one of her crazy thoughts when she heard someone yelling.

"Jaaack! What are you doing here?" Hannah said.

"Picking you up, silly."

Sunny missed the puzzled look on Hannah's face.

"Thanks but I'm staying after for drama, bonehead."

Jack gave her a hug, kissed her on the forehead. "Okay then, I'll be back later. Have fun."

She returned his hug and ran off shouting, "Love ya, bonehead!"

Jack looked at Sunny with a brilliant smile, "Looks like there's an empty seat in my car. Wanna ride?"

Sunny didn't hesitate to accept. She was thrilled to jump into the seat. He got behind the wheel and dropped his keys on the floor mat. He was relieved that she had accepted his offer but he was also a little nervous. He could feel the air change when they were contained in this small space. He hoped that Sunny didn't realize he knew Hannah was staying after and tried to *bump* into Sunny.

Sunny studied Jack as he took his place in the driver's seat. She was trying to fight the urge to run her hand through his brown, wavy hair. He smelled delicious. The electricity in the car was more intense than the other night by the pool. She was positive that if they touched she would get a shock. Just watching him get in the car and fidget with the keys made her feel woozy. He turned his head in her direction with that beautiful smile and the dancing stars in his eyes and her insides liquefied.

"Where to?"

"Anywhere you want! Out loud she gave him her address. Suddenly she wished she lived in New Jersey."

"Tell me about Sunshine."

"What do you want to know?"

"Everything."

Sunny flashed her most dazzling smile.

"I was born July third at 4:03 a.m. I was six pounds seven ounces and the most beautiful baby anyone had ever seen. You may ask my family. They will confirm that."

Jack chuckled. "Okay, okay you can skip some stuff but now I know when your birthday is!"

"I'm an only child. My parents were high school sweethearts when my mom got pregnant. My dad finished high school but my mom quit to get married and have me."

She turned her body in the seat so she could face Jack. "I think that's why my mom keeps stressing to me how important school and college are. I get it. I can't imagine having a baby right now."

Jack kept glancing at her as she spoke. He wished he could drive around for hours and listen to this beautiful girl's life story.

"I can't imagine how hard that must have been for your parents. I just finished my first year of college and there is no way I am ready to be a father."

"Right? Do you like college?"

"Yes, I really love it, even all the studying. What about you? Do you want to go to college?"

"Yes I do, I want to be a nurse and make my parents very proud of me. I want to get the education they didn't have the opportunity to."

He listened to every word that came from those lips he wanted to kiss. She seemed so together, not at all like other girls her age. She was smart, beautiful and so genuine it made him want to protect her. His feelings were not just physical, they were emotional too. This was foreign territory and he was having trouble getting a handle on it. Jack encouraged Sunny to go on because he loved listening. So she did.

"I love Fire Island anytime of the year, star gazing and my parents."

"I really enjoy star gazing too. My dad bought me a telescope when I was five years old and pointed out all of the constellations. It is still one of my favorite things to do."

"Is that why you sat by me at the party, to watch the stars?"

Jack took his eyes off the road to look at Sunny for a minute. "One of the reasons."

"…and the other?"

He started laughing. "You won't believe me if I told you."

Enjoying this game and joining his laughter she said, "I bet I will, try me."

"You bumped into me earlier in the night and when I looked at you I wanted to meet you."

"No way, I don't even remember bumping into anyone." Jack could hear the surprise in her voice.

"I think you were busy trying to keep up with the guy on your arm. I thought he was your boyfriend and was relieved when you told me you were with Kate."

Sunny didn't want to ruin the mood with her Teddy story so she kept the conversation about them. "I am pretty sure we were destined to meet, Jack; two-star gazers meet under the night sky."

Laughter filled the car.

"My mom would bring me into the yard to look at the night sky. We tried to count the stars or try and find constellations. Together we recited *Star light, star bright, first star I see tonight wish I may wish I might have this wish I wished tonight.* Kate learned to love it by default."

She giggled. "I thought the night we met; Kate sent you to check on me at the pool."

"When I saw you there I thought it was my chance to meet you. I was drawn to you. Maybe the stars wanted us to meet."

They arrived at her house much faster than either of them wanted. Not wanting their time to end Sunny invited Jack in.

As he opened her car door for her he said, "I would love to come in."

They sat at the table. Jack took Sunny's hand in his. "Why would you need checking on?"

Sunny was momentarily puzzled until she realized he meant the night by the pool.

"My boyfriend and I had just broken up at the party and I wanted some time alone to gather my thoughts."

"So I guess I had good timing," Jack said as he gave her hand a squeeze. "Are you still broken up?" Jack asked but was afraid of the answer.

"Yes. We are done for good. He is not the person I thought he was."

Jack was surprised at how relieved he was. They sat there taking each other in. Jack told Sunny about his family.

"My mom and dad are old fashioned. They're a little like the Cunningham's from Happy Days."

"Oh no, the Fonz isn't going to bust in here is he?" Sunny tried to control her giggle.

Jack really liked the sound of her giggle. "No, I am pretty sure he's not. My mom is always home baking, volunteering her time to the PTA and other local charities."

"She really does sound like Mrs. Cunningham."

"My dad works in the bank on Sunrise Highway and Hannah is my only sibling. My family is just your typical, boring family."

"Your family sounds wonderful and not boring at all. Your sister seems adorable too. Where do you go to school?"

"I go to Syracuse University. It is upstate."

"What are you going to school for Jack?"

"I am studying to be an architect. One day I am going to design buildings and homes. I love to sketch out designs all the time and one day I will design and build my dream home."

Jack and Sunny felt like they could have sat there forever, exploring each other. It felt so familiar, so right. Sunny was talking about nursing schools she might be interested in and Jack couldn't tear his attention away from her. The only thing that broke the spell was the sound of footsteps on the porch. Sunny's mom entered the house and was surprised to see a stranger at her table. Jack immediately stood up and extended his hand to Joann and introduced himself before Sunny had a chance. Sunny smiled knowing her mother would be impressed by that.

"Pleased to meet you, Mrs.?" He looked to Joann and then to Sunny when he realized he didn't know their last name.

"Marino, Mrs. Marino. Nice to meet you, as well. New friend, Sunny?" she said looking at her daughter with a raised eyebrow and smirk.

"Yes, Mom. I met Jack the other night at the party. I saw him at school today and he gave me a ride home."

Joann wasn't crazy about Sunny taking rides from people. She left it alone believing she was healing a broken heart. Joann was pleased that Sunny didn't seem as affected as she had thought and she wondered if it had to do with this young man sitting in her kitchen.

First impression of him was good, she liked that he greeted her in such a respectful way. Her husband would be impressed as well. Gary Marino was very protective of his daughter and was not a fan of "that boy" as he had called Teddy. Joann went about her business in the kitchen and kept one ear to the conversation at the table. It wasn't eavesdropping exactly…more like making sure her daughter was okay. Joann sensed their connection and it worried her.

Jack and Sunny chatted for a little while longer when Jack realized it really was time to pick Hannah up. He stood up, reluctant to go.

"I would love to take you out this weekend, Sunny Marino." He looked to Joann at the sink and asked, "Would that be okay Mrs. Marino?"

Before turning to look at him, Joann smiled to herself. She liked this young man, "That would be fine with me as long as Sunny would like to." She also thought to herself that he had better be for real or he will have her to answer to.

"Absolutely!" Sunny beamed.

"I'll call you tomorrow and we can make plans for a real date."

Jack extended his hand to Joann.

"It was nice to meet you and thank you." Then he looked back to Sunny and said, "I'll talk to you tomorrow and I am really glad I met you too!"

Sunny thought she must be dreaming, this felt surreal, but she could see him, touch him and smell him. He was real. He was glad he met her! WOW! She was glad he couldn't really see inside of her head because he would see millions of mini Sunnys running around inside of her head and screaming "he is so great" over and over again.

Chapter 5

Kate called Sunny after dinner.

"Hello and how did you get home, you weren't on the bus, I had to sit alone."

"Oh, Jack drove me home," Sunny said nonchalantly.

"WHAT? You need to start talking, Marino, and don't stop until I know everything! Spill it all." Kate was practically yelling.

Sunny didn't leave out one detail.

"Wait did you know he was coming to pick you up?" Kate managed to interrupt Sunny's story.

Sunny explained how he was there to pick up his sister. Kate thought that was a little too convenient but was so happy for her friend. She really thought that she would be consoling her this week not talking about someone new.

When Sunny finished, Kate said, "Okay when do I get to meet my future brother-in-law?" The two giggled as Sunny went on about Jack. Sunny's excitement was contagious, Kate was just as excited.

"I am making a bowl of ice cream. If you run, the bowl I just made for you won't melt." Sunny hung up and bolted out the door.

They ate their ice cream and made plans for the week. They talked about when they should go to Ocean Beach and meet with the ice cream store owner to figure out their summer schedules. They decided to take the ferry on Sunday to meet with Mr. Muncey. They also decided to hang out on the beach for a couple of hours if the weather was nice enough.

"Almost summer!" they said in unison.

Jack called on Tuesday to give Sunny all the date details. He said he would pick her up at seven and that she should dress casual. And he asked if she liked adventures. The rest of the week seemed to drag along. Sunny was anticipating her weekend date and she was daydreaming in all of her classes. She let her mind wander off to picnics, movies, strolls along the beach she wondered where Jack would take her.

FINALLY Saturday was here. Sunny tried on ten different outfits before she settled on the one she wore. She had on jeans, a purple button-down blouse and purple sneakers to match. She brushed her hair and pulled it back in a ponytail. She leaned close to the mirror as she put her mascara on. She gave herself one last mirror check, added lip gloss and was content. She was heading down the stairs when she heard the doorbell ring. Her dad answered the door. Gary eyed the man at his door suspiciously.

Jack extended his hand and said, "You must be Mr. Marino, I am Jack Johnson, it's a pleasure to meet you."

Sunny's dad took the offered hand and replied, "Nice to meet you too. Please come in."

When Jack stepped into the house he saw Sunny on the stairs and hoped that Mr. Marino hadn't heard his sharp intake of breath. If he saw her come toward him a million times he would never tire of it. She looked amazing. Purple was her color. It made her hair glow or maybe it was just her. He started to recognize that pull inside of him when he saw her. He could feel his heart being squeezed inside his chest. Sunny unleashed a smile that stopped time.

"Hello, Jack."

"Hello to you."

Gary asked Jack to have a seat and gestured toward the living room. Jack took the cue and sat down. "So did you meet my daughter at school, Jack?"

"No sir, we met at a party last weekend," Jack said.

"Do you go to the same school here in town?" Gary asked.

"No, sir, I have just finished my first year of college, I attend Syracuse University." As Jack was answering the questions he felt the need to sit up a little taller and became nervous.

He wasn't sure what Mr. Marino knew about him and he wanted to make sure he didn't give him the wrong impression.

"Exactly how old are you?"

"I am eighteen, Mr. Marino."

He wanted Sunny's father to like him so he did his best to answer the questions, look him in the eye, be respectful and let him know his intentions were good. He didn't want Gary to think he was too old to date his daughter just because he was in college. Gary seemed satisfied with Jack's answers and told them to have a good time reminding Sunny that her curfew was 11:00 pm.

"Thank you, sir, have a good night," Jack said as he opened the door for Sunny. "I will make sure to have Sunny home on time."

Sunny turned back and gave her dad a hug. "See you at eleven!"

Sunny still had no clue where they were going but truth be told, she didn't care. She was happy just driving around with Jack. As Jack drove she noticed his jaw looked tight and she assumed it had to do with her father's inquisition. She studied his face as he drove to their destination, committing every line and dimple to memory. She longed to reach out and touch his face but did not want to distract him.

She was so enthralled by him she was surprised when Jack said, "We're here." He still looked apprehensive as he gauged her reaction to their destination.

Sunny looked up and let out a squeal of joy.

"Roller skating, I love to skate!" She jumped out of the car before Jack could even make an attempt at chivalry.

Sunny's enthusiasm eased Jack's nerves. He came around to her side of the car and took her hand to head in. The smile that spread across his face made Sunny realize he was worried about *her* reaction.

"Oh, Jack, this is the best. Kate and I were regulars here all the time. Actually, I'm not sure why we stopped." They'd only known each other for one week but she felt like Jack already knew her better than Teddy ever did.

"I always loved coming here too and I just felt like this was where our official first date should be." Jack mused over the fact that they enjoyed many of the same things. It was like they were connected on another level. His favorite things were her favorites too.

As they walked hand in hand into the roller rink they both felt the electricity between them. It felt like thousands of butterflies were fluttering around her belly. Sunny could not believe that she was on an actual real date with Mr. Star Gazing, Ocean Eyes! She hoped she wouldn't fall and make a fool of herself in front of Jack. She wanted him to like her as much as she liked him. She had no worries in that department.

As they put on the rented skates the smell of popcorn invaded their nostrils. Sunny couldn't even think about food right now. Jack took her hand and they entered the skate area. Sunny was a little shaky at first but quickly regained her skating legs. They rolled together over the well-worn wood floor. The disco ball in the center cast a multi colored glow all over Jack and it made him look more handsome.

Her confidence grew and she sped up a little. They made their first lap around to walk this way. Jack was a great skater. He was graceful. He glided across the floor and the words that came to Sunny's mind were *drop dead gorgeous*. As Jack watched Sunny skate toward him he thought there was not a girl in this place who could hold a candle to her. Watching her left him breathless, and he knew he would go to the end of the Earth to make her happy.

Jack had a few girlfriends during high school, nice girls whose company he enjoyed, but not once did he feel the kind of feelings he had for Sunny. It was a little scary, good scary. He wanted to be with her, to protect her and make her happy. He was in unfamiliar territory and was unsure of how to deal with these feelings that were firing off in his head and heart.

They were skating side by side when Jack sped up and turned to skate backwards so he could watch Sunny as the music changed to *Juke Box Hero*. She got caught up watching him sing as he skated backwards. Sunny could not contain her laughter and she lost her balance and fell flat on her bottom. She hit the floor with a solid thud. When the immediate shock wore off, she started laughing again. Jack's face went from happy singing to fright to relief. He rushed to her side and helped her back up.

"Are you okay?"

"I am, maybe a little embarrassed, but not hurt." Sunny giggled.

"Are you sure, Sunny? You are really okay?"

"Really, let's just skate some more," Sunny replied.

"Well, I'm not going to let that happen again. Take my hands."

He grabbed both of Sunny's hands and skated backwards guiding her along the rink. Sunny thought she should have fallen sooner because right here, right now this felt so right, so wonderful. This was the best date a girl could ask for. She was afraid that her face was going to split in two because she couldn't stop smiling at this beautiful man leading her around.

Chapter 6

Sunny and Jack took a break from skating and went to the concession for something to eat. Jack bought them each a hot dog and they sat on the bench thigh to thigh, eating and watching the other skaters go by.

"Are you having a good time?"

"Jack, this is the best date ever, I love every minute of this night, even my fall. Thank you so much for bringing me here."

Jack was about to lean in and kiss her when the lights dimmed and the DJ announced that it was couples skate time.

Jack reached for Sunny's hand and said, "May I have this skate?"

"I would love to," she said to him. And skate anywhere with you she said, to herself.

They entered the skate area and *Dancing in the Moonlight* started playing. Could this night get any better? They held hands as they skated around and around. Jack brought Sunny's hand to his lips and gently kissed it.

"Thank you for saying yes and being my best date ever; I have enjoyed every minute with you, Sunny Marino." She was a goner. She would follow Jack Johnson anywhere.

The song changed again but the DJ kept couples skate going with *Baby I Love Your Way.* Sunny chuckled to herself thinking of her heart to heart with Peter Frampton in her bedroom. She felt completely different than the girl who talked with him. Jack sang his own version of the lyrics in his head. "Sunny, I love your way, every day." They were falling hard for each other.

They skated until the rink closed for the evening at 10:00 pm. Jack was unsure of what to do because the last thing he wanted was to bring Sunny home late but he also wasn't ready for the evening to end. So he took her down to the bay, close to her home. There was a parking lot at the end of a road that overlooked the Great South Bay. It was very romantic and you could see Fire Island, where Sunny spent her summers, on a clear night. Yes, this was the perfect way to finish the date. Jack parked the car and the couple went and sat on the sand. The evening was cool and clear and the stars were as bright as the night they met. "This is such a great spot, Jack, the perfect end, to a perfect night. Thank you again for tonight."

"It was my pleasure. I had a *really* good time too."

Jack put his arm around Sunny, they simultaneously gasped when their skin made contact. Every nerve ending jumped to attention. Sunny leaned into Jack and he slipped her arm across his stomach. They sat in each other's embrace for several minutes. Jack could not resist anymore. He needed to kiss her now. He leaned in and brushed his lips against Sunny's. It was a kiss as gentle as butterfly's wings and teeming with emotion. Sunny leaned in further and they both rose to their knees for a deeper kiss. They held each other close, kissing under the stars as their lives became as entwined as their bodies. The stars smiled down on them.

Jack pulled himself up and said, "If I expect to get you home on time, we have to go now."

Reluctantly Sunny agreed. "You're right. I don't like being late either." When they pulled up to Sunny's house Jack got out and opened the door for Sunny.

He walked her to her front door, took her face in his hands and placed a kiss on her lips. "Goodnight, Sunny Marino. I will talk to you tomorrow."

She held him tight. "Yes, you most certainly will."

Chapter 7

On Sunday, Kate and Sunny went to Fire Island as planned to secure their summer schedules at the ice cream parlor. They met with Mr. Muncey, who was able to schedule them more often when they were going to be on the island for the month and adjusted their times for when they were back on the mainland. He remembered when they were little girls and would come in with their families for ice cream and he was pleased to hire them when they became teenagers. This might be the last summer they would be able to work for him because next year they would be getting ready for college. Mr. Muncey was proud of Sunny and Kate and would be sad when they moved on. He hoped they would come back even if it was just to visit him.

It was not a great beach day, but after sorting out their summer work plans, the girls were in the mood to sit on the beach for a while anyway.

The minute their butts hit the sand Kate said, "Spill it, Marino. I want all the particulars of the date."

Sunny blushed just thinking about Jack and their date last night. "Oh, Kate, it was everything. He is totally awesome and I want to be with him every minute."

"Wow, Sun, I have never seen you like this. What the heck?" Kate's eyes widened as she spoke.

"I know, I can't describe it, but I feel as though he has a direct line inside my head. He knows all of my favorite things. It's like he can see my soul."

"Whoa, Sunny, are you for real?"

"Yeah, I thought I loved Teddy but now I think I just really liked him a lot and that it was cool being the girlfriend of the track star. But this thing with Jack is so different, it is so much more. It should be weird because I just broke up with Teddy and I met Jack minutes afterward, but I feel like I was supposed to meet him. Kind of like it was fate or written in the stars."

"I am so glad you didn't get to go all the way with Teddy. I am also glad he is over. You never talked about Teddy the way you talk about Jack."

"Maybe I needed to be with Teddy to get to Jack. I stayed up thinking about it all night because I don't want to repeat history but I have this feeling that I don't have to worry because Jack would never hurt me. He makes me feel safe. Does that sound stupid?"

"Not at all," Kate said wistfully. "It makes me want to find my Jack."

"You will, Clara Katherine, you will." Kate threw a shell at her friend.

Kate put her arms around Sunny. "C'mon let's catch the next ferry, Sunshine Rey." The girls walked to the ferry arm in arm.

Kate's mom, Florence Ackers, was waiting in the lot when the ferry arrived. She was always punctual. As they climbed into the backseat of her car, the girls were chatting away about their schedules and what stores got a facelift over the winter and if anything changed in Ocean Beach at all.

Florence loved listening to these two go on and on. As teenage girls went, Kate and Sunny were the best. Both of them were kind people, good friends and hard workers. And they each already knew where they wanted to go to college and what they wanted to do after that. Florence knew firsthand not all teenage girls had it together like these two. Her coworker's daughter Corinne was always getting into some kind of trouble and caused her mother worry all the time. Florence was thankful that Kate and Sunny were not like that.

When they dropped Sunny off, she yelled, "See you tomorrow and thanks for the ride," as she ran up the porch steps.

The phone started ringing as Sunny bounded through the door. She yelled, "got it!" She barely gasped out a hello.

"Hello, Sunny. Couldn't wait to talk to me, could ya?"

"What?" Sunny said puzzled.

"You sound like you just ran around the block. I would like to think you were running to get the phone just so you could talk to me." Sunny could hear the smile in Jack's voice and started laughing.

"You caught me. I had been waiting all day for this call and just left to get an ice cream. I heard the phone around the block, and I ran my parents over to get to talk to you."

"Good, I'm glad to hear it. I waited for the right moment to call. What are you doing right now?"

"Talking to you," Sunny said with a giggle.

"All right I asked for that. I mean do you have any plans for tonight? I would like to see you again and I wouldn't mind kissing those lips again either." Sunny could feel the heat rising in her cheeks at the thought of his lips on hers again.

She became embarrassed with her parents in the next room and whispered, "You should come over right now. I would not mind kissing you again. It was pretty nice."

Jack told her he would be there in a little while and they hung up. Sunny ran in to her parents' room, told them Jack was coming over and then ran up the stairs to get ready.

She quickly brushed her teeth, washed her face, brushed her hair and put on some makeup. At the last minute she changed into a Rolling Stones shirt that her parents bought her at their last concert. It had the same big mouth logo as the poster on her wall. Yes, her parents went without her and all she got was this T-shirt. She loved it anyway. They enjoyed the same music as their daughter, which was unusual, but Joann and Gary were young parents and music enthusiasts. Music was always wafting through the Marino home. Sunny appreciated all kinds of music because of her parents, not just typical teenaged pop. She even got to experience a Tom Jones concert with her grandmother and two of her friends. It was unusual! But she had a great time with them.

Jack pulled up exactly twenty minutes later. He came to the door wearing a Rolling Stones T-shirt that he looked delicious in. They burst into laughter when they saw each other. As Joann walked to the door, she asked what was so funny and they faced her.

She joined the laughter. "So we're all Rolling Stones fans. Good to know," Joann said. "You are certainly welcome here anytime if you like The Stones!"

Jack entered the house, followed Joann and Sunny into the kitchen and greeted Gary with a handshake. Sunny invited Jack to sit outside with her. Sunny told Jack all about her day. What her summer schedule was and how she and Kate would be on Fire Island for the month of July, but that she'd be home a lot more in August. She was going on and on when she realized Jack had grown quiet.

"What's wrong, Jack?"

"I didn't realize you would be away for the whole month of July; I won't get to see you."

"Oh no, I didn't think of that yet. Do you work in the summer?"

"Yes, I work in the hardware store and mow lawns." Jack tried to hide the disappointment out of his voice.

"You must have days off. You can stay at the beach house with us. That would be fantastic!" She practically jumped out of her seat. "Say yes, Jack. Come to the beach house this summer." Her zeal was infectious and Jack found himself agreeing even though he wasn't sure how he would work it out. Jack would figure out a way to get there. He wasn't sure what his parents would say either or her parents for that matter. He knew his parents would think staying there was inappropriate. This wasn't going to be easy but it would be so worth it.

"Tell me about your job at the hardware store."

"There's not much to tell. I sweep, stock the shelves and help customers."

"I love talking to all the people when they come into the ice cream shop and I love the owner too, he's so nice."

"I have to like the owner of the hardware store, he's my uncle." Jack laughed as he spoke. "I have worked there since I was fourteen. My uncle John is really cool and I like working with him."

"I get it, I love my job at Sprinkles, I can't believe I get paid to scoop ice cream and eat it too."

Jack had an incredulous look on his face. "Do you eat ice cream every day?"

A giggle burst out, "Yup, every day. I eat it for breakfast too sometimes."

"Well, at least it has milk in it," Jack said as he joined her laughter.

Just sitting chatting with each other was so natural and easy. They continued getting to know each other.

"Tell me more about your sister Hannah."

Jack beamed when he spoke about her. "Hannah is a great kid. She is fourteen. We are very close and she really misses me when I am in school. That is the hardest part about going away to college, missing the day-to-day stuff. I love being a part of that and I try to call her all the time. But it's not the same."

Sunny thought that Hannah was lucky to have Jack. Kate and her brother weren't even almost that close. "Tell me about your parents."

"My parents are just regular parents. My mom stays at home and takes care of everything. She can make a swan out of a napkin and make it look like it's as important as making electricity and she can cook and serve a meal that is worthy of a president. She is awesome. I think Hannah has a lot of my mom in her."

"I would love to see one of her swan napkins, it sounds so cool. What is your dad like?"

"Dad is quiet. He comes home, turns on the TV or goes out to the garage and putters around. He loves to tinker with stuff too. He's cool, you can ask him anything and if he doesn't have the answer he will find it." Jack was holding Sunny's hand as he spoke running his thumb back and forth over the top of her hand.

"Do you have a best friend?" Sunny's face was serious.

"I have friends of course, but one isn't closer than any other one."

"I'd like to apply for the job," Sunny said raising her hand like she was in school.

"What job?" Jack looked at her curiously.

"The best friend job, silly."

"Oh, but I thought you already had a best friend job with Kate," Jack said catching on.

"It's true. That position is already filled, but I am a very good candidate for more than one position. There's enough Sunny for both jobs!"

"I don't think I could ever get enough Sunny," Jack lifted her hand to his lips and kissed it.

Sunny's insides started doing flips even simple little words coming out of his mouth could make her crazy. She was longing to kiss him but her parents were right inside so she had to settle for thinking about kissing him. By the time Jack said she had the job. She really had no idea what he was talking about.

He started laughing. "The best friend job, it's all yours."

Gary came outside and invited Jack to stay for dinner. Jack said he would love to but he needed to use the phone to let his mom know he would not be home for dinner. Gary smiled and showed him to the phone. They all sat down for dinner and chatted with an ease like people who had known each other for a long time. Later that evening Joann and Gary sat outside and discussed how smitten their daughter was with Jack. They certainly liked Jack more than Teddy.

"Jack seems like a genuine young man. Not like he is putting on a show for us like that last one." Gary held his coffee cup to take a sip as he spoke.

"Believe me I am glad to see him go but I am worried our little girl is falling hard and fast for Jack." Gary took her hand and squeezed it.

"Sunny will be fine, she's our girl."

Chapter 8

The next few weeks of school went by in a blur. Jack and Sunny saw each other almost every day. Sunny even got to spend some time getting to know Hannah and she liked her a lot. She had lots of friends and was always going off somewhere or having them over. She had the same aura as her brother and people were drawn to them.

Sunny had dinner at Jack's house two weeks after he had dinner with her parents. Sunny had a chance to get to know his parents a little, they were more reserved then her parents. The meal was delicious and Jack's mom was an amazing cook.

The two grew closer by the day. In a short amount of time they knew each other's dreams and desires. Most of all they desired each other. They could spend hours kissing and often did. They would park in their special place, the beach at the end of the block where they had their first real kiss and sat together under the stars.

Sunny hung on Jack's every word when he talked about the house he wanted to design one day. He knew he would find the perfect piece of land and to build his dream house on. She hoped to be part of that dream as much as he wanted her to be a part of it. She could imagine living in that house with him if she wanted, but she was done making plans like that. She learned her lesson with Teddy and was taking things day by day without grandiose dreams of her future with Jack

Sunny told Jack that the day they met *You're My Best Friend* was playing while she got ready, and that she believed that it was a sign they would meet. She would quote song lyrics and make theme songs for events all the time.

"Apparently that's our theme song then," Jack said as he took her face in his hands and kissed her.

She placed her hands on his arms and met his kiss and said, "I guess it is, because it's true Jack. You are my best friend, Kate is truly my best girl but she is more my sister than a friend, I can't ever imagine life without her and I love her so much, but you are different. You are more."

"Oh, Sunny you are so much more to me too. Sometimes I feel like my heart is going to burst with what I feel for you."

He took her into his arms and kissed her with a passion she felt in her toes. She wrapped her arms around his back and held him so tight a piece of paper couldn't fit between them. Feeling stirred in Sunny that made her want to do more than kiss but as always Jack was the gentleman. He stopped before the point of no return, when they were both breathless like they had just run a marathon.

July approached faster than Jack was ready for and he was sad that he would not get to see Sunny every day. The good news was that he would be able to spend Fourth of July weekend with the Marino's and Ackers' on Fire Island. They would be celebrating Sunny's Birthday that weekend too. Joann invited Jack to come for the entire weekend. Even though Jack was eighteen, he was completely respectful to his parents. He asked Joann if she wouldn't mind speaking with his parents about the weekend. Joann reassured them the sleeping arrangements would be appropriate. She also let his mom know what a kind young man she thought Jack was.

Charlotte Johnson liked Joann immediately after that call. The families seemed to have shared the same values and that was important to the Johnson family. Jack didn't care if he had to sleep on the sand, as long as he got to see Sunny. He was able to get the time off from the hardware store and arranged his lawn maintenance jobs around the weekend. Most of his customers wanted their lawns cut before the holiday weekend anyway.

Sunny left for Fire Island the weekend after school let out. Jack drove her to the ferry, which was a big help to her family because their car was packed with all the stuff they were bringing to the house. Jack didn't mind because it meant he could spend every last minute with her. She kissed him goodbye not caring who saw, walked down the dock and stopped just before getting on the boat.

Turning back she yelled. "One week, I'll be waiting for your ferry!"

Jack worked his butt off for the next three days so he didn't have time to miss Sunny much. After work he walked up and down the mall looking for the perfect birthday present. He knew what he wanted to get Sunny for her birthday and made it his mission to find it. He tucked the small box in his bag, the anticipation excruciating.

Sunny kept busy unpacking and working at the ice cream shop in the week leading up to Jack's arrival, but she was standing on the dock ten minutes before Jack's ferry was due. He was on the top deck watching for her to come into view as the ferry approached. Just as he could recognize the girl he had missed so much in such a short time, the ferry turned to dock properly. He made his way down to the gangway in two seconds. Sunny was practically jumping out of her skin waiting for the other passengers to get out of the way. It was in that split second she knew what the stars already did. She loved him with her whole being. Yes, her heart was all his, forever.

Finally, there he was! "Jack!" she screamed and ran to him nearly knocking over a boy with his wagon.

She launched herself into his arms and he dropped his duffle bag to catch her. He lifted her off her feet and they kissed like they hadn't seen each other for a year. As they kissed he spun her around so her feet flew through the air.

Eventually her feet touched the ground, she looked into his ocean eyes and said, "Jack Johnson, I love you so much, it hurts!"

"Oh, Sunshine, I love you heart and soul." It didn't feel awkward or wrong, it felt so right and they didn't care who could hear them. They kissed one more time and walked to the beach house with their arms around each other stopping every few steps to kiss again and again.

"By the way, Sunny, your lips taste like ice cream," she giggled and it stopped his heart.

"I just got off work and it's hard not to take a little taste before I go."

"I think I am starting to like ice cream more and more, especially when I can taste it on your lips." They both broke into laughter as they got to the door.

Kate's dad, Bill, was on the porch. "What is so funny, you two?"

Before Jack could say anything Sunny blurted out, "We just thought it was hysterical how much we both like ice cream!"

Jack remembered his manners and extended his hand to Bill. "Nice to see you again, Mr. Ackers. Thank you for including me on your family vacation."

"Your very welcome, Jack, and please call me Bill. We will be under the same roof for the weekend and I don't want to feel old," he said with a big smile. Kate definitely got her smile from him.

Jack was unsure of what to expect of his first Fire Island experience. The Ackers/Marino home was not big by any means, but it was so cozy and beachy, you couldn't help but feel relaxed and happy. In the tiny open kitchen sat Joann and Florence chatting over tea. Jack gave both the ladies a hug. He then walked over to Gary who was sitting on one of the mismatched sofas and shook his hand. After the pleasantries he was unsure of where he should put his bag down or sit. Florence stood and said, "Jack, follow me and I'll show you where to put your stuff." Jack did and she led him into a nook in the back of the house. There was only enough room for the daybed tucked into it. Florence motioned toward the bed. "It's all yours, Jack."

Jack smiled. "This is great, thank you Mrs. Ackers."

"It's Florence, Jack, and the bathroom is on the right when you need it."

Jack put his bag on the bed and followed Florence back to the living room to join everyone. Joann smiled at Jack.

"Welcome to Fire Island, Jack. The best place on earth! Five minutes to town or five minutes to the beach, whatever strikes your fancy is just a short walk away. Not a car around and shoes not necessary anywhere. Paradise." Joann made sweeping motions with her arms as she spoke.

Kate was still working at the ice cream shop so Sunny decided to give Jack a tour of her summer town.

"Get your bathing suit on but put a shirt on too, you can get arrested here for walking around without a shirt over your suit." Jack looked at Sunny like she was joking but she assured him that there were many rules here in Ocean Beach and he needed to be sure to follow them. "Stick with me and I'll keep you out of the big house."

They walked back toward the town first. "Here is the pizzeria, you can eat your slice right in front of the store, but one foot on the sidewalk and it's the big house for you."

"What other rules should I know?"

"We only have one weekend so I won't give you the whole list, just the most important ones. Don't eat in the streets, don't drink in town, you know about the bathing suit thing. I saved the most important rule for last. Kiss me at every corner."

"I think I like this place. Maybe I should stay." And he lowered his lips to hers.

Sunny and Jack continued their tour of the town. Sunny pointed out all of her favorite spots. "This is the restaurant that my parents took me to on our very first trip. I loved it because I could play in the sand until my meal came, best place ever."

"Wait." Jack grabbed Sunny's hand as she was heading off into another direction. "Corner! I want my kiss so I don't get arrested."

They walked to the bay beach. "Directly across from here is our beach on the mainland, isn't that cool?" Sunny smothered his yes with a kiss.

As they made their way to the ocean Sunny and Jack popped into Sprinkles for a quick hi to Kate.

"I love it here, Sunny, you make me want to stay all summer."

"Wait until we get to the beach!" Sunny grabbed his hand and ran the rest of the way to the water's edge. The water was still pretty cold. Goose bumps crawled up her legs as the surf splashed up. She took her cover-up off and tossed it next to the beach bag. Jack stopped dead in his tracks. Sunny was in a pale pink bikini. It was the first time he saw so much of her. The dryness in his mouth left him speechless. He just took his shirt off.

The sight of Jack's bare chest took Sunny by surprise. She had run her hands up and down his back before and could feel how muscular he was but seeing it up close was a whole different thing. Sunny fought the urge to run kisses up and down his stomach. She was so distracted by her wicked thoughts a wave came and knocked her off her feet. That bare chest could be dangerous. It was so cold and Jack was laughing so hard she couldn't resist she grabbed him around the waist and pulled him into the surf with her.

"Still funny wise guy?"

Jack grabbed her and jumped into the cold water. "Yep, still funny!"

They played around for a couple of minutes but decided it was too cold to stay in so they headed for the towels and wrapped themselves up to dry off and warm up.

Jack looked at Sunny with a raised eyebrow. "You love me so much it hurts?"

She smiled and nodded her head as she pointed to her heart. "Jack, I know it was only a few days but I felt like it was a year not being able to see you. As the ferry was pulling in I realized that you are so important to me, that you are everything and I love you so much that I couldn't help but blurt it out. I didn't care whether or not you would say it back I just wanted you to know how I felt."

"It felt natural for me to say it too, not just because you said it but because it is how I feel. You are part of me. I know it in my heart and in my soul and I can't imagine how I'm going to go back to school and not see you, I can't even figure out how I am going to make the rest of July without you. I go to bed thinking of you and you are the first thought I have in the morning. I love you!"

They accepted each other unconditionally. Sunny wasn't afraid to let her feelings show and Jack didn't have be macho, they were just who they were. Jack went over to the beach bag and fumbled around in it. Sunny was puzzled as he took out a small box she didn't recognize. Jack had one of his belly liquefying smiles as he handed her the box.

"What is this and where did it come from?" Sunny asked.

"I brought it with me and slipped it into the bag on our way out. Happy Birthday, Sunshine!"

In her excitement at seeing Jack and meeting him at the ferry she forgot it was her birthday. Her birthday wish had already been granted today. She tore open the wrapping anyway and inside was a silver bracelet with a dangling roller skate. She threw her arms around him. "Thank you! Every time I wear this I will remember the best first date ever."

Jack smiled. "That was my intention."

That night the whole group celebrated Sunny's birthday with ice cream cake and music. They laughed and danced around the house and it was one of the best nights Jack had ever had. It was captivating to be with this group of people. They embraced Jack and he felt he was becoming part of something very special.

The rest of the weekend went by fast and Jack, Sunny and Kate did everything they could squeeze into one weekend. They went boogie boarding, watched the Fourth of July wagon parade, took a boat ride and went clamming. They spent their nights on the beach stargazing. The Fire Island night sky was dazzling. The stars reflected off the ocean and made it glisten.

Jack was so happy to get to know Kate better too. He wanted to like her for Sunny and found it hard not to anyway. She was fun and she was so good to Sunny he would be crazy not to like her. Even her family was great. Jack also got to bond with Sunny's parents, he liked them even more than he did before and they were so kind to him and he was grateful to be there. But the time came at last; he had to leave and Sunny was walking him to the ferry with glassy eyes.

"As much as I love it here, I want to get on that ferry with you, Jack."

"I know, but this might be your last summer here like this for a while and I want you to enjoy it. So get over here and hug me."

She did as she was told and kissed him so hard her lips hurt. He pulled back and gently held her chin while looking into her beautiful face.

"Sunny, promise me you will enjoy the rest of this month and I promise you I will come back when I can." They both kept their word.

Jack visited several more times, just for the day and Sunny came back to the mainland with her dad on her day off. Jack came out to help the families pack and rode the ferry back at month's end.

Chapter 9

August brought back Sunny and Jack's home routines. They worked at their respective jobs, spent all their free time together and spent plenty of time with Kate too. Jack enjoyed Kate's company and loved the way she and Sunny interacted. It made him feel special to be a part of both of them. Sometimes he would bring Hannah along as well. They went to the beach together, played mini golf and went to the drive-in. Jack even gave Sunny some driving lessons when she got her license.

With only one week left before Jack went back to school the couple knew summer was coming to an end. During that week he wanted to spend as much time with Sunny as he could. Kate and Hannah were scarce that last week. Jack was pretty sure they planned it that way and he was grateful to both of them. He knew Sunny would need them when he left. Sunny didn't talk about his leaving, but he thought it was because it upset her too much. Jack picked Sunny up and took her to their special place. From his trunk, he took out a duffle bag, the same one he brought to Fire Island. In his bag were a blanket, sandwiches, fruit and lemonade. Sunny threw her arms around his neck and proclaimed he was the best boyfriend in the history of all boyfriends.

Jack answered her by embracing her and placing a slow, sensuous kiss on her lips. He let his tongue explore her mouth and she melted in his arms. The pair came back to earth and realized they were not alone on the beach. They pulled apart and sat down to enjoy their meal.

Jack and Sunny ate and neither spoke. They just watched the water. Jack broke the silence.

"Sun, I have to leave in a couple of days and I'm scared of how much I will miss you. I will miss this." He waved his hand around. "I will miss touching your face and looking into your eyes. I was thinking that maybe I could transfer to a local school and finish."

Sunny held his gaze while she spoke. "You can't do that. You need to finish what you started. Besides I will apply to your school's nursing program so we will be together next year. I am going to miss you so much it hurts, the same way I love you."

"I don't think I can wait that long; I'm scared."

"We can do this; we are that strong. Nothing will stand in our way. We will call as much as we can and I will write to you all the time."

"I love your confidence as much as I love you, Sunshine."

"I have the best idea. I'll pick a song to let you know how I'm feeling. We can listen to it at the same time, look at the stars and feel each other. We will stay connected."

She was trying to convince herself as she said it. She wanted to be strong for Jack. If he thought she was okay, it would be easier for him. He deserved that from her. She decided it would be okay for her to plan their future a little bit by looking into the nursing program at Jack's school.

Even though she was no longer making long term plans she believed this was a smart move. She needed to go to college, so she could plan that. She could become a nurse and be near the man she loved so much at the same time. Yes, that was okay.

"I like that idea. We will make this work. Talking this out made me feel better. You make me feel better, Sun."

Sunny snuggled up against Jack and his arms encircled her. They watched sky change colors as the sun set. As the colors faded into the bay, their emotions rose. When the sun disappeared into the water the tears in Sunny's eyes began to fall. She could hold it back no longer, the thought of not seeing Jack took its' toll on her emotions and she let it flow. Jack held her tight to him knowing there was no stopping it. He actually wanted to join her. Jack did his best to keep strong for Sunny, but the tears flowed down his cheeks too.

To console her, he spoke softly in her ear and placed kisses on the top of her head.

"I am so glad we talked about this. I feel better just sharing my fears with you."

"I feel the same way. Let's always be honest and not hold anything back."

"I can do that. I find it so easy to share my innermost feelings with you. Sometimes I can't remember not having you to talk to, I feel like you have always been here for me. You have made me so happy and I promise to always be there for you. I love you heart and soul."

The sky grew darker as Sunny's tears receded and acceptance resonated within them. This was not the end of the world and they would make the best of the last few days of their summer. And they did. Sunny and Jack spent every minute they could together talking, laughing, making memories and kissing.

The day arrived. The Johnson's car was packed with all of Jack's necessities for school. The Camaro was tucked into the garage for the semester. Jack and Sunny felt as dismal as the humid, rainy morning. They stood in the driveway holding hands, facing each other, eyes locked. Jack's dad had the car running and the radio was on. His mom locked the door of the house and looked at Jack.

"I'm sorry you two but we have to get on the road soon."

At the same time, *You're My Best Friend* started playing on the radio of the Johnson's car. Sunny smiled with a tear in her eye and said, "Look, our song is playing and it's a sign everything is going to be fine, so from now on whenever I hear this song I will know it's all going to work out. You're the best friend that I have ever had."

Jack replied, "You're MY Sunshine and my feelings are true; I really love you." When he got in the car he had a lump in his throat.

Chapter 10

The start of Sunny's senior year was exciting even though some of the thrill was dampened by Jack's absence. Sunny and Kate sat for senior pictures and joined the planning committees for senior trip and prom. They filled out their college applications. Sunny knew that only one college would be the right one for her, but she went through the motions anyway. Kate wanted to stay close to home and chose only local schools with teaching programs. She only applied to one "sleep away" school, as she called it. Kate was nervous to go away and she thought that Jack was brave being so far away from home. She wanted to be an elementary school teacher, preferably at the school in town where she and Sunny attended.

Sunny's counselor told her the nursing program at Jack's school was a highly regarded program. Although it would not have mattered either way, knowing this made her even more excited to apply there. The other applications that Sunny filled out were to local colleges. She was just as much a homebody as her friend Kate. It was her missing Jack so much that allowed her to even consider going farther away. She knew she would feel at home with Jack nearby.

Sunny poured herself into her classes every day and would come home to check the mail for a letter from Jack. They agreed to talk every Thursday at 9:00 pm. Jack would get rid of anyone that went near the one payphone in the hall of the dorm. After a while everyone knew that Jack was talking to his girl and left it open for him. Sunny would call Jack so they didn't have to be interrupted repeatedly for more change, it wasted valuable talk time. During their weekly phone calls they would choose their song of the week. The selections went from upbeat songs that put a smile on their faces to sappy love songs when they were lonesome for each other. Some of the weekly selections included *Miss You, Walk This Way, Unforgettable and Kiss on My List.* They even agreed on a listening time, Sunday nights were song times.

Sometimes Jack would request it on the college radio station and dedicate to Sunny. Even though Sunny could not hear it Jack liked doing it. One night after song time, Sunny was listening to Psychic Sundays on the radio. She had the urge to call in to the show and gave in to it.

The DJ answered and she nervously said, "I would like to speak to the Psychic."

She was placed on hold for what seemed like hours. Sunny was losing her nerve and started to think she was being silly.

She was about to hang up when she heard, "You're on the air with Psychic Mike. What's your question?"

Startled Sunny said, "Hi, I'm Sunny and I was wondering if you can see what college I am going to go to?"

"Is there a male figure in your family who has passed?"

Sunny pondered a second, "Yes, yes my grandfather."

The Psychic went on, "He had trouble with his lungs and he could not breathe or speak before he went to the other side. He wants you to know that he is pain free and can breathe easily now. He thanks you for sitting with him all of those nights. He always knew you were there and he said strawberry was his favorite."

Tears streamed down Sunny's face. Her grandfather died when she was twelve, in her house, he had lung cancer and was brought home for his final weeks. Sunny would sit next to him in his hospital bed, watch TV with him and bring him ice cream, vanilla ice cream, chocolate ice cream but mostly strawberry ice cream. She would have to sneak the ice cream because her mother told her it wasn't good for him. But he loved it so much she would never deny him. She would tell him all about her day, what she and Kate did and anything else she could think of. That time with him she wouldn't trade for anything. One morning as she was leaving for school, she went in to kiss him on his cheek like she did each day since he had been there, and it felt different. It was so cold. She gently called to him with no response. She knew he was gone. How could anyone else know this but Papa? She never told anyone about the ice cream she brought him.

"Sunny, are you still with us?"

"Yes, sorry my grandfather lived in my house until he died and I snuck him ice cream at night."

Psychic Mike chuckled. "That explains it, I deliver the message and I don't always understand but as long as you do that's what matters. Your grandfather says you will need to be strong soon and not give in to your despair. You will be challenged and if you stay strong and depend on those who love you you'll be okay. He wants you to know that he watches over you and he is proud. He is adamant about you needing to place your trust in those who love you. He warns you not to give in to your fears. Remember he is with you."

"Thank you," was all Sunny could manage before she hung up.

She didn't even realize that her actual question went unanswered. She was rocked her to her core. It sounded crazy but that was definitely her grandfather speaking to her. There were just some things you can't figure out and this was one of them. Kate and Sunny had always half believed in Psychic Mike, but tonight Sunny really believed. Her hand still held the phone and it started ringing, Sunny nearly jumped out of her skin.

"Sunny, HOLY CRAP, I just heard that whole call. Was that stuff true?"

"Kate. Oh my God. It is all true. I used to sneak ice cream into Papa and sit with him. I am totally freaked out."

Kate and Sunny talked about the phone call until they were barely able to keep their eyes open anymore.

Chapter 11

Parents' weekend at Jack's school was in October and the Johnson's invited Sunny. Gary and Joann had several long discussions regarding the trip and finally decided they would allow it. Sunny had been working so hard in school and they knew how much she missed Jack. She was so excited she couldn't stop hugging both of her parents. As much as they like Jack they were worried that Sunny was so in love with him she was going to put her dreams on hold to be with him. That was not the kind of girl they wanted her to be – yes they wanted her to find love and share her life with someone, but they also wanted her to be a strong, independent woman with her own career and mind. She had been trying so very hard to do her best in spite of missing Jack so much. That fact aided in their decision-making process.

Gary dropped Sunny off at the Johnson's house Saturday morning and they were off. Hannah couldn't join them because she had a big soccer game. She was staying with a teammate for the weekend. The anticipation of seeing Jack had Sunny fidgeting in the back seat. She was trying hard to appear calm to the Johnson's, but this ride was taking so long. Where in the world was this school,

California? At last they arrived on the campus and Sunny was looking all around trying to spot her best friend. They parked and started toward an old brick building. She assumed that Mr. and Mrs. Johnson knew where to go and she followed right behind them.

She was doing her best to talk herself into making sure she didn't embarrass anyone. She was afraid the moment she saw him she would scream and jump into his arms. Sunny was taking deep breaths when familiar arms wrapped around her from behind. All of the calming breaths were forgotten and she trembled while trying to turn her body toward the love of her life. She succeeded and they were entwined with one another in an embrace until Mr. Johnson cleared his throat. Reluctantly Jack released his girl, hugged and kissed his parents, encircled Sunny's waist with his arm, holding her tight to his side.

"Hi, Mom; Hi, Dad, I have missed you guys."

His dad said, "I can see that, Jack," and they all laughed.

They continued the walk toward the building, which turned out to be the student center. There was a big welcome reception for all the families. Jack's mom and dad made their way over to the refreshment table. Sunny couldn't even think of putting anything past her lips except for Jack. She was crawling out of her skin longing to kiss him. Jack exchanged some small talk with some of the students running the event, never once removing his arm from her waist. Jack could feel her tremble and knew he needed to get her alone. He introduced Sunny to several different people whose names she would never recall.

Her mind was wandering up and down his body. She wanted to grab his face and smash his lips against her own while wrapping her whole body around him. Just when Sunny thought she would die from not being able to kiss Jack, he looked into her eyes and asked her to take a walk with him. She would walk with him anywhere.

He whisked her out the door and to the side of the building. There between two large shrubs he sandwiched her against the wall and kissed her with his whole being. They poured their hearts out to each other in that kiss. The angst of the past few weeks was released in that exchange. At first they held on to one another tightly, then, they let their hands explore each other, their lips still locked. Sunny ran her hands up and down his back and through his hair. Jack had one hand on the back of her neck and the other around her waist holding her firmly to him. Sunny felt like she could melt right into his body, her knees were weak and her insides liquefied. They had to come up for air eventually and when they did they were breathing so hard it sounded like gasps. They stared at each other until their breathing was more controlled and Jack said, "Oh…my…God…I missed you."

"I kinda missed you too," she replied and then broke into those giggles that set his heart aflame.

He cupped her face with his hands and placed sweet kisses all over her face. She rested her hands on his arms gently kneading them. They stood for a while just taking each other in.

"Do we need to go back in to your parents, Jack?"

"No, I arranged for them to have a special tour of the campus so we can have some time together."

"They're okay with that? I feel funny, it's your weekend to visit them and they came all this way to have someone else give them a campus tour."

Jack's sexy grin let Sunny know it was okay. "They had the grand tour last year with me, but they don't mind going again because they knew how much we missed each other."

"Oh Jack, they are terrific. I was so antsy to see you I could hardly sit still in the car and they never said a word. I was afraid I would scream your name and jump into your arms and embarrass them when I saw you."

Jack brushed her golden-brown hair away from her face and said, "Scream away if you want but it will be very hard to hear while I'm doing this," and he started kissing her again.

She wanted to scream again but in a different way this time. When they had their fill for the time being he took her hand.

"Follow me."

"Anywhere, anytime, my love, just lead the way."

Jack gave Sunny the brief tour of the campus and then he showed her his dorm room. It was smaller than she had imagined. There was a twin bed against the far wall that had a brown comforter on it and the area around the bed was tidy. The other side had another twin bed that was in total disarray with clothing, sheets and wrappers all over it.

Jack had a huge boyish grin on as he extended his arms out and said, "Guess which one is mine?"

Sunny hoped that it was the tidy bed. She had never thought about this side of Jack and had a fleeting moment of worry that he was a slob. That thought was quickly erased from her memory as Jack knocked her down on one of the beds and jumped over her laughing.

"I bet you're thankful I'm the clean one!"

"I was worried for a minute but right now I really don't care."

Jack hovered over her propped up on his arms, dazzling smile staring down at her, she couldn't help but return that smile. They were so happy to see each other.

The air in the room started to charge, they felt it in their breath. Their expressions melted into pure desire. They had never been alone in a room on a bed. Jack lowered himself onto Sunny and she put her hands on his face and lifted her lips to his. It was a slow, deliberate movement that made his toes curl.

Sunny wrapped her legs around his waist which brought his full weight on top of her. Jack raised himself up so he could see his beautiful girlfriend. They let their inhibitions free and explored one another's bodies. Jack ran his hand slowly from her knee. He caressed the curve of her waist with one hand while easing the other hand inside her shirt. He undid her buttons slowly and kissed each newly exposed bit of skin each time. He traced the outline of her bra with feather light kisses. She squirmed with desire. He positioned his body alongside Sunny so he could let his finger roam along the top lacey part of her bra making a "v" across the front of her and slipped his hand in to cup her breast. Sunny had never felt anything so exquisite. She wanted to feel more. She pulled him back over her and ran her hands all the way from his shoulder down his back and she ran them over his and stopped on his behind. She felt brazen, she pulled him back on top of her and could feel how much he wanted her, which sent her over the edge.

That's when Jack came back to the present. He could have gotten lost in her, but it was far from the right time or place. He loved her far too much for their first time to be in a heated rush when anyone could walk right in. It would be perfect when the time was right.

He raised himself on his arms and studied Sunny's face as she was regaining her composure. Her expression asked the question she didn't have to.

Jack whispered, "You are my Sunshine and when we make love it will be spectacular, not in a half clean room. I want to make love to you under the stars like the night we met. I couldn't help myself because I missed you so much, but we should go and meet up with my parents."

She nodded, "I know, you're right but I want you so much. I want to climb right into your body. Seeing you made me miss you more and I just want all of you right now!"

"Oh, Sun, you have all of me, heart and soul, remember?"

"I do, but I want more of you." She grabbed him back and started kissing him again.

In one swift movement Jack flipped on his back with Sunny in his arms so she was astride him. She giggled and playfully grabbed his arms pinning them over his head.

"Listen up, Jack Johnson, I will have more of you soon. So accept it." With that she got up smoothed out her clothes and looked around the room. "Where is your mirror?"

"Don't have one here, but you don't need it, I will fix you up," he said as he stood up and walked to her. He brushed her hair with his hands until she looked presentable again. "Okay gorgeous, let's go find my parents."

They walked around campus hand in hand until the met back up with Jack's mom and dad. Mr. Johnson looked the both of them over carefully and suddenly Sunny felt extremely self-conscious. Maybe it was guilt in part for what she had been doing with his son and more for what she wanted to do to him.

She looked away and said, "I feel bad Hannah is missing this. She would have loved it!"

Mrs. Johnson said, "I know but she was so torn between wanting to see her big brother and her soccer tournament."

"I see where I stand. That gets me right here." He pointed toward his heart.

Sunny, Jack and his parents spent the next two days attending all of the events that the college planned. On their last night together, they had an early dinner at a local restaurant so they could get on the road. Sunny could hardly eat and mostly pushed her food around on her plate. She didn't want to seem ungrateful but every bite felt like it burned her stomach like acid. Jack noticed her demeanor and placed a hand on her leg under the table. He gave it a gentle squeeze and a look that eased her. In a few minutes they would have to say goodbye again. After dinner they brought Jack back to his dorm and his parents hugged and kissed him.

His mom started to cry and took his dad's hand and said, "Let's wait in the car."

Her tears made Sunny's fall as well. Jack took her sad face in his hands and wiped the tears away with his thumbs. He placed his lips over hers.

"I love you and I will miss you. When you get home tonight I want you to listen to our song and I'll do the same, and we will go to sleep thinking of this weekend."

"I will. I love you and I miss you already." She walked slowly to the car with tears streaming down her face.

Sunny curled up in the back seat as the car was pulling away. As they made their way to the highway Sunny realized the college radio station was on. It sounded as though Mrs. Johnson may have raised the volume too, was she crying out loud? Oh no. The next thing she heard made her smile and cry at the same time.

The radio DJ said, "This next song is a special dedication to Sunny from Jack."

It was *Baby Hold On*. She looked to the people in the front seat who could not contain their wide grins.

"I'm afraid I have really got it bad for your son." Sunny whispered from the back seat. "There is no going back. I love him."

Chapter 12

Jack made a decision after that weekend to really put his nose to the grindstone and try and finish school early. He believed he could increase the amount of classes each semester to graduate early. The only problem he could foresee was if Sunny attended his school then they would be in the same predicament. He would figure something out. He needed and wanted to be back on Long Island with his girl. He could see himself spending his life with her. Now when he dreamed of building his house, she was on the porch with him when it was done. He knew that this was the girl he was going to marry. He was positive she would be his life partner. He started making plans for their future. When he finished school and had a good job he was going to ask her to be his wife. He didn't worry about Sunny finishing college; he could wait as long as she needed.

While Jack studied harder, Sunny kept herself busy. She missed Jack terribly but she was starting to cope with it better. Her parents were glad she wasn't moping around so much. Sunny even took Hannah out once in a while to the mall or for ice cream. Jack was thrilled that his sister and girlfriend were growing close.

Jack and Sunny would write letters to each other constantly. They still had their weekly rituals too, but the letters made them feel more connected. Sunny would run to the mailbox to check it every day. She pulled out that familiar envelope out and held it close to her chest envisioning Jack's lips as he licked envelope and his face as he wrote the words on the page. She would sit on the porch steps quietly and read the words he put there for her eyes only.

My Only Sunshine,

It's one in the morning and I have been studying my butt off because midterms are next week. I keep losing my concentration because every time I close my eyes I see your lips and wish they were on mine. I want to hold you in my arms and drink in the scent of you. I want to lay on the beach and look at the stars with you by my side. I count the days until I can really touch you. I will be home for Thanksgiving and I can't wait to feast my eyes on you. I can't decide what I want to do first, hug you or kiss you so I think I will do both. Your love keeps me going, I want to complete my education so I can come back to you.

I hang out with friends when I'm not studying or sit in class. but my mind always goes back to you. I am hopelessly in love and I wouldn't change a thing.

How is your week? Hannah told me that you two went to the mall and she had a great time with you. Thank you for hanging out with her. She really enjoys it. How's Kate? Has she found Mr. Awesome yet? Sorry there's only one of me and I'm yours! Anyway tell her hold out for Mr. Perfect because she deserves it. Maybe I should just pick someone out because I'm going to have to hang around with him too I don't want him to be an idiot! Hahaha I will talk to you on Thursday and I think I know what song I am going to pick this week, but you'll have to wait!

Love you heart and soul,
Jack

That week the song Jack picked was *Bad Case of Loving You*. Her parents had it in their huge record collection. Sunny still went to the record store to buy the song. Her parents never said no if she asked for money to buy music.

Sunny saved every single letter Jack wrote to her. Sometimes when missing Jack was unbearable, she would reread his letters to soothe her heart for the moment. She still had trouble wrapping her mind around how deep her love was for him in such a short time. She actually felt bad for Teddy because she didn't even come close to loving him. He moved on too and had a new girl to parade around. She didn't harbor any resentment toward him even after what happened at that party. She really did want him to be happy.

Dear Jack, best boyfriend ever,
Well my love, Kate and I just made the final plans for our senior trip. We are going skiing in February. It's my first time but Kate has done it before. I am excited about the trip and I hope that doesn't make you feel bad. I will still miss the daylights out of you, but I'm looking forward to it. I would like to go skiing with you one day. Do you ski?

Never mind. You can learn. I will even teach you because I'm sure I will be an expert by the end of the trip!

I too have been counting the days until Thanksgiving when I can see that handsome face. I want to grab you and run my fingers through your hair and kiss your whole face. I might even put some peanut butter in your dimple and kiss it out. The first time we met I thought of that and I would love to try it. You game? I want to celebrate your birthday too! I have a special present for you. Guess what it is? You'll have to wait.

Jack, there's something else. Sometimes I worry about us. What if you meet someone at school and you want to be with her because she is THERE and I am not? I know you will say that you love me but sometimes I just worry. Sorry.

I will see you at Thanksgiving and my worries will disappear. It is the distance that gives me doubt.

Dying from the pain of loving you so much,
Sunny aka Your Only Sunshine.

When Jack read this, he did not understand where her doubt came from. Why would she believe anyone could take his attention from her? He needed to call her tonight and reassure her she was the only one for him. He went down the hall to the phone and dialed her number.

"Hi, Mr. Marino, this is Jack. May I speak with Sunny?"

"Sorry, Jack, but she isn't here. She is with Kate somewhere. Who knows with those two?"

"Okay, please let her know I called and if she could return my call tonight, that would be great."

"Jack, is everything okay?" Mr. Marino sounded genuinely concerned for him.

"Yes, sir, it just something important I need to tell Sunny so I will be up waiting for her call."

"Will do, Jack. You take care of yourself. Goodbye."

"Thank you, I will. Bye." Jack hung up worried about his girl.

Jack sat in the hall by the phone. His attempts at studying were worthless so he had given up and camped out to wait for the phone to ring. When it did he jumped to his feet and knocked the phone out of its cradle. It bobbled in his hands for a few seconds and when he finally gained control of it, he brought it to his ear. "Hello."

"Jack, it's me. What's wrong?"

"It's you, Sun. I just read your letter and I don't understand why you doubt my love for you. I don't even notice other girls. You are the only one I see. I want you to feel confident that I am not going to let you go or walk away from you. YOU ARE MY SUNSHINE and without you I would be in the darkness. Do you understand me? YOU are my girl." He emphasized the YOU by nearly yelling it.

Sunny was dumbfounded. She immediately was sorry that she even wrote that to him. He sounded angry; she hadn't wanted to upset him.

"Jack, I'm so sorry, I didn't want to make you mad. I start missing you so much and let my mind wander and I start thinking what if…" he interrupted her.

"Sunny, I am not mad at you. I want to make sure you know my intentions. You are my one and only. There could be a hundred other girls but they are not you."

"I like being your one and only."

"I could search the world and I would not find another girl that makes me feel the way you do. So, knock it off! No more what-ifs. If you start feeling like that again, call me. If you don't, I *will* be mad at you. Does that make sense in that pretty little head of yours?"

She started giggling and broke into tears at the same time. "It makes sense. No more what-ifs. I won't let my mind go there. I can't wait to see you. One more week to Thanksgiving and we get to be in the same room. Imagine that!"

"Oh I have been imagining that for quite some time now and I have been imagining the ways I can be in the same room with you. I also might just bring a whole jar of peanut butter!"

Sunny laughed so hard she dropped the phone. "So you are game! Now I am even more anxious to see you."

"I am more than game. I'm ready, willing and able. So what's my present?"

"I am not telling you; you will have to wait until you get home. I want to see your face when you un-wrap it," she said excitedly.

Just hearing Jack's voice was magical for her. "Good night, Jack Johnson, thank you for calling and making me cry and laugh and love you more!"

"Good night, Sunny, and remember YOU ARE THE ONLY GIRL FOR ME. I love you."

Sunny skipped off to bed and was asleep as soon as her head hit the pillow. She dreamt of Jack and of a house by the sea.

Chapter 13

Jack arrived home the Tuesday before Thanksgiving. He had gotten a ride from a friend to Penn Station and took a train home. Sunny jumped at the chance to pick him up. When she heard the train approach the station, she got out of the car. He made his way through the crowd of people leaving the train and dropped his bags down the moment he saw her already running toward him. She leapt into his arms and he caught her as she wrapped her legs around his waist. They embraced and kissed just as promised and the world around them melted away. The sound of applause brought them back to earth. Sunny blushed and Jack put her down. He took a bow.

"I really missed my girl, Happy Thanksgiving everyone!" He waved and took Sunny's hand.

Sunny got behind the wheel of her mom's car and Jack got in the passenger seat. He looked over at her with the biggest smile, the kind of smile that made Sunny want to jump him all over again.

"This is a first, Miss Marino. Now I get to watch you instead of the road."

"No, it's not. You gave me driving lessons, silly."

"True but I was looking at the road and your technique. Now I can study your face, watch your hands hold the steering wheel, study the muscle in your leg that flexes when you step on the brake. Oh, this is going to be a nice treat for me."

"Well, I'm glad you are pleased. It is my goal this weekend to please you, in more ways than one."

She put the car in reverse with a satisfied smirk on her face. Now it was Jack's turn to be stunned. What exactly did she mean? Should he ask or leave it alone? No, he would wait, he was going to enjoy this ride.

"Do you need to go straight home? Is your mom expecting you?"

"No love, she doesn't expect me until after dinner, I'm all yours for a couple of hours."

The idea of having Jack for hours, alone, made it hard for her to concentrate on driving. She headed right to their special place. They were the only ones in the lot as Sunny pulled into a parking spot. It was too chilly to get out of the car, but she had a better idea anyway. She climbed across the car and onto his lap. She sat astride him, took his face into her hands and planted kisses all over his face.

He pulled her to him so tight and returned her kisses. He slowly ran his hands up and down her back. Sunny hovered over his lips while staring into his green eyes. Sunny nearly combusted by the desirous look in Jack's eyes. She put both hands into his hair and pulled his mouth to hers. She kissed him like her life depended on it. Jack returned her affection with his own desire. They were a tangled bundle of limbs but they couldn't stop. Jack put his hand inside Sunny's shirt, touching the skin on her back. He traced the vertebrae on her back with his fingers weaving around each one. She moaned from the touch.

"Jack, I want you so much; I'm so happy to be in your arms." She started to open his coat and shirt.

"Believe me I want you so bad I can taste it."

"I taste it too and I like it." She was still working on his shirt. He held her hands still on his buttons.

"But not here, we need to slow down because I think I am getting lost in you. I could get lost forever with you." His words spoke to her soul.

"Why do you always have to be so chivalrous? So kind, so wonderful, blah, blah, blah."

"That's me, and I am all yours."

"Oh, Jack, I'm all yours too. I love you so much."

Sometimes she hated this kind, wonderful, chivalrous man. He was good inside and out and he was all hers.

"Jack, let's stay here for a while; I just like having you close enough to touch. I am content knowing you are in my reach. It soothes my soul."

They sat holding each other with Sunny still on Jack's lap. Her head was on his chest and her arms held him to her. He rested his face on her head so he could plant a kiss on her or inhale her scent whenever he wanted. In each other's arms they were home.

Jack broke the silence. "It's getting cold. Maybe we should get going."

"I'll start the car to warm us up I don't want to share you yet."

Sunny climbed back into the driver's seat and started the engine. She snuggled back into his side and they gazed out onto the bay as the heater got going.

"This is what I miss most. We can just sit here in each other's arms. We have a problem though."

"What could that be?" Sunny liked this game, she batted her eyelashes.

"What you are thinking."

"Oh really, what am I thinking?"

"You want us to stay like this forever and some other very scandalous thoughts."

He pulled her back onto his lap, this time she was across his legs with her back against the passenger door.

"True and stop reading my mind." She giggled. "Do you have any peanut butter?"

Jack laughed, patting himself down. "Not with me, but we can fix that!" His expression turned serious. "I'm not reading your mind, it's like I can feel what you think. You send out this vibe and I hope it's just me who knows what it is."

Sunny feigned a horrified look. "I hope it's not out there for everyone to read, I'll have to be careful. Besides I think you are the only one who knows what is going on inside my head."

"I had better be the only one," he replied in his sternest voice, and then smiled and kissed her cheek. She turned her head to meet his lips. "Know what I am thinking now, Psychic Jack?"

"Yep, and it's not going to happen here, Sunshine. When the time is right, it will be as special as it should be. You are too precious to have your first time be a bumbling mess in a car. When it's right, we will know it."

She would have made love to him right here, right now but she wanted it to be special too. You only get one first time. Then she started wondering, was Jack a virgin too? Probably not, he was a college guy and she guessed he must have done it.

Jack watched the joy melting from her face and he knew what was worrying her. "It will be my first time too. I thought it was too important to do it casually. I think it should be special with someone I love, and that someone is definitely you."

Sunny was delighted by his words again and agreed he was right.

Chapter 14

On Thanksgiving, they stayed with their families, but they planned on spending the entire next day together. Sunny got up early on Friday and helped her mother put the house back together after hosting the rest of their family for Thanksgiving dinner. Joann was exhausted from all of the holiday festivities so she didn't mind giving Sunny the car for the day. Jack's Camaro was off the road until the summer. It was silly to keep it on the road during the school term and while she missed his car, she didn't mind picking him up.

Sunny arrived at Jack's house before eleven and knocked on the door. Hannah opened the door yelling.

"It's Sunny," as she motioned her inside.

Jack came down the stairs wearing soft, faded Levi's that hugged his bottom half just right and a plain white T-shirt that clung to his torso. As he put a sweatshirt on over his head, his muscles rippled through his shirt. Sunny had to look away to stop a fire burning her from the inside out. She didn't even hear Hannah asking where they were off to.

Jack looked at Sunny and then to Hannah with half a smile on his lips and said, "None of your business. Today is

Sunny-and-Jack day and we don't need little sisters poking their nose around."

He grabbed Hannah and put her in a headlock, poked her in the nose and kissed the top of her head.

"Whatever, bonehead, more leftovers for me." She stomped off toward the kitchen.

Jack shouted after her, "Save me a turkey sandwich, brat."

She laughed back at him, "We'll see."

Jack grabbed his jacket and Sunny's hand. "Ready?"

"Absolutely," Sunny beamed.

"First things first, I'm hungry. Let's get something to eat," Jack said.

"Okay, where to, the diner, Ground Round or Carvel?" Sunny asked with a huge grin.

"Is there ever a time when you couldn't eat ice cream, woman?"

Sunny shrugged. "I haven't found one yet, but I would give up any meal including breakfast for ice cream. Why do you think I got a job at Sprinkles?"

"Sorry no ice cream today. I want real food. Let's go to the diner." He opened her car door even though she was the driver and closed it after she was in.

As Jack devoured the cheeseburger he ordered, Sunny enjoyed her hot fudge sundae and they discussed what they wanted to do for the rest of the day. Jack had something really special planned for the evening, so Sunny got to choose how they'd spend the afternoon. She knew just what she wanted to do. She didn't tell him she just started driving. She got onto the Robert Moses Causeway and headed south and Jack had an idea of where they were headed.

Sunny drove the car to Field 5 of Robert Moses State Park. It was the closest parking lot to the towns of Fire Island. You could walk to Ocean Beach if you parked there. It was a beautiful day for November and Sunny brought two blankets: one to sit on and one to snuggle in. They sat side by side.

Sunny asked, "Are you ready for your birthday present?"

He held out his hand and closed his eyes and said, "Yep, I want my present."

Sunny produced a wooden box from her beach bag, placed it in Jack's hand and told him to open his eyes. It was hand-painted dark blue with stars on it. It was beautiful and smooth and it glistened in the sun. Now Sunny was on her knees watching Jack examine this piece of art.

Jack looked at her in awe. "Did you make this?"

Sunny was beaming. "Yes. I painted it and I put all of the stars on it. Look inside, C'mon."

She was bouncing on her knees like a little child and Jack was caught in her spell. He lifted the hinged lid and inside was a cassette tape in a case. It had a paper jacket and handwritten it said:

Our Story
As told by music…
Made with love for Jack
From Sunny

The cassette jacket had a picture of the beach drawn in colored pencil and the artwork was amazing.

He asked again, "You made this whole thing?"

"Yes, my dad helped me with some of the wood work, but I sanded it all until it was smooth and painted the whole thing. I wrote down every song we ever listened to together and put them all on one tape so you can listen whenever you want, and I made an extra for me."

It was the most loving and thoughtful gift he had ever gotten. He gently placed it down before guiding Sunny onto her back and kissing her soft and sweet.

"Thank you for the best gift I ever got. You are quite an artist; you never cease to amaze me, Sunny Marino."

"You're very welcome. It was easy to do because I made it with love."

They stayed at the beach for a while longer watching the submarine races until it became too chilly to stay.

Their evening event started at 8:00 p.m. and Jack had already cleared it with the Marino's to keep Sunny out past her curfew. Jack was very tightlipped about the night, it reminded Sunny of their first date. The journey took about 30 minutes and Sunny wasn't even sure where they were by the time Jack parked the car. He came around to her side, opened her door and extended his hand.

"You are going to love this," and they walked toward the building arm in arm.

As they approached the building, Sunny saw the sign; <u>Vanderbuilt Planetarium.</u>

"No Way! The planetarium! I have been dying to come here!" She nearly ran the rest of the way into the building.

They found an empty pair of plush seats that reclined so you could see the dome above. The house lights went off sending the room into total darkness as the music started along with the light show. The lights danced to the beat of songs such as *Another One Bites the Dust, Long Time and Fool in the Rain.* Sunny and Jack held hands with their heads leaning toward each other. After the light show the dome changed to a magnificent night sky and then a thunderstorm rolled in. It even rained in the planetarium. It was a perfect night. Sunny and Jack would remember this night forever.

As they were leaving the planetarium after the show, Sunny looked at Jack.

"Wouldn't it be unbelievable to have a ceiling like that in your own house? I would adore that. Wouldn't you Jack?"

He smiled at her and nodded but it sparked an idea, something he would keep in his memory for later. It was late, so he drove straight to his house since they had Sunny's car. But he wasn't crazy about Sunny driving home so late by herself, he made her promise to call when she got home. He waited by the phone so it wouldn't disturb his parents. Before the phone made one full ring Jack lifted it off the receiver and whispered *hello*.

"Hi you, I am home safe and sound."

"I am glad to hear that." He was still whispering.

"I really love that you could not go to bed until you knew that. You sound very sexy when you whisper."

"Maybe I should do it more often."

Sunny could hear the smile in is voice. "Thanks for a great time. The planetarium was so cool and I would love to go there again."

"You are very welcome and the pleasure was all mine. As a matter of fact the whole day was great."

"I loved spending the entire day with you. Happy birthday, Jack."

"I love my birthday present; I love you and I will fall asleep listening to all of our songs tonight."

"Well I can't let you listen alone, so I will listen until I fall asleep wishing I was lying next to you. Good night and I love you, Jack."

"I love you, Sunny. See you tomorrow… Oh how I like being able to say that!" They slept that night dreaming of starry nights in each other's arms listening to their songs.

The next day was gloomy so they decided to rent some movies and watch them at Jack's house. Hannah convinced her mom that she needed to go shopping and Mr. Johnson was tinkering with things in the garage so it was like they had the house to themselves. Sunny curled up against Jack to watch a movie.

"Jack, I know we haven't been together that long but I feel like it is where we belong, with each other."

"You know I feel the same way, Sunny. Where is this going?"

"I think we should take us to the next level." Sunny wouldn't look at Jack when she spoke.

"What next level?" He wasn't letting her off easy and had a smirk on his face.

"Jack, I want to be *with* you."

He gave her arm a squeeze and said, "It feels like you are." Jack wasn't giving an inch. He was in a playful mood and loved watching Sunny try and make him understand.

"Jack, please I am being serious."

"Me too, I am *with* you, Sunshine." He kissed her. "You feel that? That was me being with you."

She looked around the house and was confident that his dad was out in the garage, so she straddled his lap and grabbed his shoulders.

"Stop and don't make me say it."

He feigned innocence. "Say what, my Sunshine?"

She smiled to herself and thought two can play this game. She kissed him slow and gentle and then deepened this kiss with a fervor that made Jack's playful attitude turn to pure desire in a nanosecond. She trailed little kisses all the way to his ear and whispered in his ear.

"I want to make love to you, Jack; every inch of you, heart and soul. Understand me now?"

Hell yes, Jack understood. If they were alone, he would have taken her right there. Instead he took both of Sunny's hands off his shoulders and lifted her onto her feet. He could not regain his composure with her on his lap. He walked over to the TV and shut it off and when he did, he could hear his father's music from the garage. Jack could make out the song too. It was one of his dad's favorites: *What a Wonderful World.* Jack focused on this for a minute or two so he could talk with Sunny without knocking her down on the couch and granting her wish.

Sunny stood there too stunned to move. Was he rejecting her? She felt so stupid now. When Jack turned around to look at Sunny, he felt like someone just punched him in the chest. He was the reason for that look and he needed to act fast. He swept her up in his arms and danced with her to his father's song. He leaned in and whispered to her.

"Let's go for a ride. Wait here a minute."

He ran out to the garage and asked his dad to borrow the car. Then he grabbed the keys and Sunny. They drove to the town marina, not their special place. He wanted to really talk to her without any distractions or interruptions and he could not trust himself at their spot. There were plenty of people at the marina. Sunny stared out the window, silent for the entire ride.

Jack parked the car, shut it off and turned his body so his back leaned against the driver's door. She still didn't move.

"Sun, look at me."

She turned to him fearful of what he was about to say.

"I want to make love to you with all of my heart and soul. I have never wanted anything so bad in my entire life. It would be easy for me to give in to my desires and take you right here and now. What I don't want is for you to regret the decision. I want you to be completely sure this is what you want too. I need to know it's not just your physical need. I want your body, mind, heart and soul. I want all of you. I need to know you are ready with every fiber of your being because this is a huge step for both of us and there is no going back. You never get your first time back and I couldn't live with myself if I hurt you or if you regretted it."

She held his gaze the entire time he spoke. He waited for her reply. He couldn't read her expression and she did not give anything away. The only sound in the car was their breathing. He went on.

"This is NOT a rejection. I know that is what you feel right now. I repeat I am NOT rejecting you I am respecting you. Sunshine, please say something."

There was a long pause and her expression started to change slightly.

"Why do you always seem to know what I am thinking, Jack?"

"When I look in your eyes it's like I can feel what you think, I can't explain it exactly," he said shrugging his shoulders.

"Yes, I do feel rejected but after everything you just said to me I'm okay with it. What I feel more now is overwhelmed with love."

He took her hands in his and kissed each one. "I'm relieved."

"You are the most incredible person I have ever met. There is probably not a guy around who would have said no to me but you did and you made me feel more loved by doing it. You are everything to me." Sunny's eyes were filling as she spoke.

"You better not be offering yourself to any other guy. That offer is mine and mine alone."

As he said the words he reached out for Sunny and pulled her across the seat onto his lap. She smiled and put her arms around his neck.

"You are the only one I would ever make that offer to. You are all mine and I am all yours."

Chapter 15

Sunny had a serious talk with her mom after Jack went back to school, she wanted birth control. Joann was momentarily speechless, but she had always let Sunny know she could come to her about anything, including this. She did not want history to repeat itself. She loved her family with all of her heart and wouldn't change anything but she had still missed out on normal teenage stuff like proms, beach dates, senior trips and girlfriend sleepovers, because she got pregnant so young.

She wanted more for her daughter. She wanted Sunny to have it all, the fun teenage stuff, love, college and fun. From the moment Joann laid eyes on her daughter and she wrapped her tiny fingers around her own, she knew that this baby was her own ray of sunshine. Joann was elated to be her mother and wanted her to have the best of both worlds, to know that same maternal love, but maybe not so soon.

Sunny's request did take her by surprise. She wasn't ready for it. Joann was also relieved to know that Sunny was still a virgin. She had her suspicions about Teddy and was glad. Joann was also so proud that Sunny came to her before she actually had intercourse.

"You have not been with Jack that long. Are you positive this is the choice you want to make?"

"Yes, Mom, he is my everything. I can't even imagine having anyone else in my life."

"I know, my love, but once you go down this path and make the choice to have sex, there is no going back. And it changes things." Sunny was smiling at her mom.

"Something funny, Sunny?"

"No, Mom, it's just that Jack said that too. I told him I was ready Thanksgiving weekend and we had a long talk about it. He wants me to be sure and he won't do anything until I am."

Joann admired his restraint; most nineteen-year-old boys would have made a different choice. She swallowed hard to push the lump in her throat down.

"I'll make an appointment for you this week, love. I am so happy that you came to me, I guess the inevitable is happening and my little ray of Sunshine is growing up."

She embraced her daughter as tears slid down her cheek. "I think Jack is a keeper. However, you should warn him that if he breaks your heart, he will have me to deal with."

The doctor visit went as expected and Sunny started taking the birth control prescribed the next day. Sunny looked forward to surprising Jack when he came home at the end of the semester.

The day Sunny had been looking forward to, had finally arrived. Jack was on his way home from school. Sunny had a romantic evening planned. Her parents had gone to the city to see a play and they were staying overnight. They had no idea Jack would be home this weekend. If they had, they most likely would have stayed home. Joann was on board with taking her daughter to get birth control but she wouldn't give her the house for the weekend to be alone with her boyfriend.

Sunny spent the whole morning getting ready for their evening. Crisp, clean sheets were on the bed, the furniture was polished and the rug vacuumed. Sunny shaved, plucked, applied facial mask and moisturizer, did her make-up, blew her hair and changed her outfit five times. She nervously looked in the mirror at the tight dark jeans she chose. She looked at her feet. She needed shoes to match the shimmering silver blouse. Sunny borrowed a pair of silver pumps from her mom's closet. One last look in the mirror, Sunny was satisfied with her outfit and with any luck she wouldn't be wearing this very long anyway.

She heard a knock at the door and ran to get it forgetting she was wearing heels. She nearly toppled over, but luckily she made it to the door without incident. Jack was standing there looking so good it should be against the law. His hair was still damp from his shower, he had on a plain white T-shirt, faded jeans and a leather jacket. He looked like a stereotypical *bad boy* but she knew better – he was good inside and out.

Jack was about to say something funny because he could hear her giggling her way to the door, but the minute he laid eyes on her he barely remembered his own name. Her shirt clung to her in all the right places and the sight of her in high heels and tight jeans made his mouth go dry. He stepped in and grabbed her. He put one arm around her waist so he could pull her tight and the other arm he placed on the back of her head so he could perfectly position his lips on hers. He kissed her with an intensity that instantly set her on fire. Sunny put both her arms around his middle holding on as if she might fall and met his kiss with the same intensity. They stood there kissing, their bodies melting into each other. When they finally stopped Sunny smiled so bright her eyes lit up.

"Miss me?"

Jack shoved his hands in his pockets, shrugged his shoulders and said, "Nah." They burst into laughter.

"You look beautiful and really hot; I couldn't even say *hi*. I just had to kiss you."

"That is perfectly okay with me. I look hot?"

He nodded his head with a smoldering look in his eyes. He whispered, "Really hot."

Sunny had a satisfied grin. Jack put his arms back around her.

"Where would you like to go?"

She looked into his eyes making sure he could read her mind and mouthed, "Right here."

His knees nearly buckled. "Are you sure, Sunny?"

She led him by the hand to her room. With wobbly legs he stepped into her room. He had never taken the time to examine her room before. Jack ran his hand across the posters of her favorite bands. He turned on the stereo and imagined her listening to their songs at night. He picked up one of the little jewelry boxes that were perfectly placed on the dresser. Jack walked over to her neatly made bed that was adorned with decorative pillows and a stuffed animal in the center. He picked the giraffe up and stroked the neck. Sunny snatched it from his hands.

"That's my Alfie. Hands off!"

"Okay, just let me know what I can touch." As soon as the words were out of his mouth he couldn't believe he said them.

Sunny threw her hands up in the air while turning around and said, "How about all of this!"

"Your wish is my command."

He closed in on her and interlocked his hands with hers, stretching her arms up over her head. He slowly ran his fingertips down the length of her arms, gazed the side of her breasts and put his hands on her waist.

He asked, "Is this okay?"

All trace of humor vanished from her eyes, only to be replaced with desire. Her mouth was dry but she managed to croak out a *yes*. Jack removed his jacket and neatly placed it on the chair never letting his eyes leave hers. This simple act was making Sunny squirm.

He cupped her face in his hands and said, "You can change your mind whenever you want. I love you and that won't change."

"I am not going to change my mind. I want this as much as I love you. Now get over here and make love to me."

Jack started kissing her again while backing her up to the bed. He gently guided her down never breaking contact with those delicious lips. They were a mass of tangled limbs and heavy breathing when Jack suddenly stopped and stood up.

"What's wrong?" Sunny nearly cried out.

Jack's mouth formed a grim line. "Sunny, I don't have a condom and I won't risk it."

She held his gaze and said, "Don't worry about it."

He looked horrified. "What do you mean don't worry? You ready to be a mom?"

"Not even a little bit, but I am on the pill so get back over here." He started to say something, but she stood up and put her face near his.

"I will tell you the whole sordid story later but right now I need your lips right here," she said as she kissed him.

"You amaze me, Sunny." He laid her back down but didn't join her.

She was the most beautiful girl he had ever seen and he was lucky enough that she loved him. He thanked his lucky stars that he went to that party and met this girl. It had been the luckiest day of his life until right now. Jack wanted nothing more than to dive right in but he also wanted to take his time and savor every moment. He removed her shoes and ran his hands up her legs until he reached the waistband of her pants. Sunny shivered. He unbuttoned them and unzipped them so slow she thought she might pass out. He pulled her pants off and looked at her lying there. He trailed kisses all the way up her legs; he had never felt anything so soft and smooth. He let his hand wander under her blouse and couldn't believe she was softer here. He gently removed her blouse too. She had the prettiest bra and panties; the sight of her had him panting.

Jack couldn't take his eyes off of Sunny and she actually enjoyed it, it felt natural. She relished every touch, every kiss. She felt like she could do this forever. She sat up and tugged at his shirt, and helped him remove it. She ran her hands over his chest. Nothing had ever felt so good. The skin-to-skin contact was electrifying. She touched the waistband of his pants and he trembled. With shaky hands he stepped back and removed his pants. Every nerve ending sizzled as the last of their clothing was shed.

She inhaled the scent of him, this was heaven. She thought, *if this felt so good what would the actual sex feel like?* He climbed up her body and they melded together. She could feel how much he wanted her. He kissed her so slow and deliberate it made Sunny quiver. She wrapped her legs around him. Jack looked into her eyes seeking her permission. She nodded and brought her hips up to meet his. He was so gentle but she winced as he entered her.

Jack nearly jumped off the bed. "Did I hurt you?"

"It hurts a little bit and feels good. Don't stop, please."

Unsure, Jack gently lay back down and caressed her face. He kissed again as he regained his composure.

"Jack, I won't break, please make love to me."

Her pleading was his undoing. It was everything she had hoped for and more. It was like your most favorite song playing while you were on the beach eating ice cream looking at the stars with the person you love with all your heart. Well, multiply that by ten thousand and that's how incredible it felt.

Afterward they were lying on their sides facing each other still trying to catch their breath.

Sunny spoke first. "I want to do that every day!"

Jack let one of his slow spreading smiles loose, the kind that crawl up his face into his eyes and make his dimple look even more edible.

"I can arrange that for you." And he got right to work granting her wish.

They snuggled together satiated. Sunny felt Jack stiffen as he turned to her.

"Tell me now about the birth control pills."

Sunny touched his face, "I talked to my mom after you went back to school and told her I was ready for this and she made an appointment with her doctor who is now my doctor. I had an exam and he prescribed them for me."

Jack rolled on his back and put his arm over his eyes. "Ugh, your mom knows what we just did?" Then he bolted upright. "Oh my God, where are you parents? Will they be home soon?"

"Relax, Jack. They won't be home until tomorrow."

He raised his eyebrows. "In that case." He pushed her back down and kissed her.

Chapter 16

Once the lovemaking floodgates opened, Sunny and Jack couldn't get enough of each other. Every possible minute they had to be alone they were. They knew their time was limited, Jack would have to go back to school before the end of January and Christmas was already just a couple of days away.

Sunny's family hosted a big Christmas Eve gathering every year. Sunny was spending the day with her mom helping around the house. She would not see Jack until Christmas night because his family spent Christmas Day at his grandmother's house. But she couldn't wait to exchange gifts with him.

At last it was time for Sunny and Jack's Christmas. They sat together on the couch in the living room. Her parents had gone to bed early, they were exhausted from the party on Christmas Eve. Jack handed her a small beautifully wrapped box.

"I want you to open my gift first."

Sunny tore the wrapping and pulled the lid of the box off. Inside was a necklace. It was a swirl of silver that thinned out toward the middle and ended with a dazzling silver star in the center.

"Jack, it's so beautiful."

"Turn it over."

The words went around the circle; *I will love you as long as the stars shine, Jack.* She threw her arms around him.

"I love it almost as much as I love you. Help me put it on, please."

She held her hair up and Jack fastened the clasp. As he did he placed gentle kisses on her neck and she felt that clench deep inside that she had become very familiar with recently. In an instant she turned and straddled his lap.

"Miss Marino, you have become a sexaholic and I love it, but this is not the place."

"C'mon, Jack, we will be so quiet and there is no way my parents are waking up. They were up until the wee hours last night, singing and dancing."

He was torn by his good sense and his desire and as Sunny ran her hands down his chest to the button of his pants. Desire won.

The joy of the holiday season intertwined into the joy of being together daily. The weeks flew by and January arrived sooner than they wanted but Jack had to go back anyway. He promised to come back for spring break. Sunny was trying to work out a way to go visit him too. They kept their song tradition going on as well. During one of their phone conversations Jack broke into *Ain't No Sunshine When She's Gone* and Sunny went to sleep that night with the biggest grin on her face. The next week she told him she missed him so much she needed *Sexual Healing.* Their little tradition eased the longing for each other somewhat and gave them something to look forward to.

Sunny came home to see a letter from Jack's school. She trembled as she opened it. Sunny was accepted to the nursing program at Jack's school and she nearly threw up she was so happy. Sunny was jumping up and down, she wanted to call Jack but knew he was in class. She called Kate. The minute she heard Kate's voice she blurted out,

"I'm in! Jack's school, I was accepted!"

Kate started screaming. "I was accepted into the teaching program here! Holy crap! We are awesome."

"I can't believe we both found out on the same day and our dreams are coming true. I can't wait to tell Jack."

"He is going to be so happy to have you there. Maybe you could share a dorm with Mr. Wonderful?"

Sunny giggled, "I'd never go to class."

It was at that moment she came up with a plan. February break was right after the senior trip. Sunny somehow convinced her parents to let her go visit Jack. She was unsure of what convinced them, but there was no way she was going to question it. She had her directions written out and set off to surprise Jack.

After some carefully crafted conversations with Jack, she was able to ascertain the exact location of his room. He chose a single room this semester and it was a different building from when Sunny had visited. She arrived late at night and made her way to the building. She found his room and thankfully the door was unlocked. She crept in and there was her man, sleeping in his bed with a pile of books on the floor next to him and one on top of the blanket. She tiptoed in and silently removed her clothing. Gingerly, she lifted the book off the blanket. And with only her bra and panties on, she slipped into bed with him. Jack stirred and she could feel his body freeze.

She wrapped her arms around him and whispered, "Surprise."

"Sunny! Oh God, please tell me I'm not dreaming. How the hell did you end up here?"

"I drove here all by myself to surprise you, did it work?"

"Best surprise ever, Sunshine," he whispered and planted a kiss on her lips. The next morning she shared her news with Jack.

"I'm in, Jack. I was accepted. Right here with you!"

His eyes widened and he let out a whoop! "We should room together and wake up like this every day."

"I would love that."

When Sunny got back from visiting Jack, she was putting her clothes away when she saw them. Her birth control pills were in the top drawer. How could she have forgotten them?

"Holy shit, that was dumb. Thank goodness it was only a weekend."

The day-to-day routines, happiness about college and Jack were all she thought about until Jack came home for spring break. Sunny and Jack were snuggling after making love. Jack was kissing the tops of her breasts.

"I think your boobs grew."

"I know, my bra feels tighter, I guess I'm having a growth spurt." Sunny giggled which Jack quieted with his mouth.

Their blissful streak continued and their love deepened.

After he went back, Sunny focused on the rest of her senior year and mainly what she would wear to the prom.

While getting ready for school one morning, every pair of pants she put on, were too tight. Twenty minutes and five pairs of pants later, she was officially late for school. She decided on a pair of elastic waistband pants making a mental note to cut back on the ice cream. When she got to school Kate was waiting for her by her locker.

"C'mon, Marino, we need to decide where we are going to shop for our prom dresses."

"I'm afraid to go, none of my pants fit me, I need to lose five pounds before I shop for my dress."

"You don't look like you put on weight, Sunny…well maybe your butt is bigger."

Sunny looked horrified, "My butt too?"

"Oh my God, I was just kidding, let's go," Kate said with disbelief.

By the time she realized what was going on with her body she was eight weeks pregnant. She decided to go to the doctor to confirm what she already knew in her heart to be true. She was so frightened. She was not ready for this; she was going to college. Jack needed to finish college. Sunny was starting to panic and she didn't share her fears with a living soul.

The doctor confirmed her worst fears. She was pregnant. The doctor brought her into his office and discussed all of her options as far as the pregnancy was concerned. He gave her pamphlets and papers with phone numbers. She left in a daze.

Sunny felt like the walls were closing in on her, so she drove to their spot. She started thinking how stupid she was to forget her pills. This one mistake could ruin their lives. Sunny was thankful that it wasn't her day to talk to Jack because she wasn't ready to talk with anyone. She needed to process this news. She sat in the car thinking for hours and she knew what she had to do.

Chapter 17

It was 8:50 p.m. on Thursday. Sunny felt sick, and not from the pregnancy. She was going to tell Jack today, and she was shaking as the minutes passed like hours until she could not delay the inevitable and dialed the number. Jack was quick to answer as usual and the happiness in his voice made her quiver and cry.

"Hey, brown eyed girl. How's my Sunshine this wonderful day?"

She swallowed hard. "Fine, Jack. How has your week been?"

"Oh, Sunny, I have had a great week and I was thinking before finals I am going to come home for the weekend and we can go skating. Or if you would rather do something else, I don't care I just want to see you."

He sounded so excited and happy and Sunny wanted nothing more than to be part of that joy but she had to burst the bubble and tell him her news.

"That sounds great, Jack, but first I want to tell…"

Jack interrupted, "I had the best thing happen today. You know that I have been taking extra classes and breaking my ass to get ahead? Well, I was offered an internship this summer and an opportunity to study abroad in ITALY! I didn't say yes because I wanted to talk to you first, and part of me doesn't want to go because I will miss you so much; it will hurt but it is such an unbelievable opportunity I am so thrilled they offered it to me. This could open doors for me and my career and that would mean great things for us. Oh my God, Sun, I am so excited! Crap, I have been going on and on. Are you still awake?"

She could hear the smile in his voice. He was so excited and she wanted to scream. Her heart broke as she realized she could not stand in the way of him realizing his dream. Sunny could not ruin this moment for Jack. He needed to go to Italy and she wasn't going to tell him tonight.

"Jack, I am so happy for you. That sounds like an opportunity you can't pass up. You need to go to Italy. I will miss the living crap out of you but, we can do this. It is way too important for you to miss. I will have so much to get ready for this summer and maybe I will work at the ice cream store again and make some money while you are away."

"You know you are the best girlfriend a guy could ever ask for? I want you to think about it some more and be sure you are okay with this."

"Jack, stop, it's okay. This is your decision. It shouldn't be based on how I'm going to miss you. It would be selfish of me to ask you to stay, and I would not do that. You need to finish school and get a great job and it seems like this will be the fast track to achieve that."

"Wow, you are mighty insightful tonight and I appreciate your honesty. I really, really want to go but I want you to be okay too."

"I'll be fine, Jack. Listen it's getting late and I want to finish some work before I go to bed. Go to Italy, everything will be okay. Goodnight, Jack, I love you."

"Sunny, wait, you wanted to say something before I started my rant."

Jack felt uneasy and thought it had something to do with Sunny's reaction to his internship.

"Just that I love you, that is all." And she hung up.

After the phone call with Jack that night, it was crystal clear that the decision she had come to was the right one. That night in the car she weighed all of her options. She had choices concerning her pregnancy, choices not everyone had. Her mother either had to get married or give her away. To her mother, giving up Sunny was not an option. For Sunny, having the baby was not an option.

Seventeen years ago, an abortion was done in some dirty back room on a folding table. Sunny never grasped what her mom was faced with when she found out she was pregnant, but she understood now. The choices she could have taken for granted were choices she was lucky to have. Sunny lived in a time when women were in charge of their own bodies and didn't have to put their lives in jeopardy if they chose not to continue their pregnancy. She didn't take the choice lightly; she accepted the responsibility of her decision or so she thought.

She told no one of her choice. She came to it alone and she would carry it out alone. Sunny thought she could terminate her pregnancy and move on with her life. Jack could finish school; she could start the nursing program and one day they would have a baby. It was more of a dream than a plan. She made an appointment to have an abortion and drove herself to the center.

Sunny sat frightened in the waiting room. When they called her name she thought of running out the door, instead she made her way to the room on unsteady legs. She could barely change her clothes; she was shaking so hard. She lay on the table, her eyes fixated on a spot on the ceiling and became mindful of the ramifications of her choice. There was no going back from here. The baby that was inside her now would be gone in a few minutes.

The doctor spoke. "You will feel a pinch and then pressure, make sure to take deep breaths..." his voice started to fade into the distance as the noise from the machine droned on and extracted the life from her body.

Sunny withdrew into herself to escape the situation. It was at that moment she felt like she was hit with a brick full of reality. As the life was removed from her body, fear and guilt replaced it. Did she just blow her only chance to be a mom? Would she ever be able to have a child? How could she be so callous? If there is a God, would He be mad at her? If God was angry with her, would He punish her and not let her have children? She felt woozy unsure if it was from the procedure or the thoughts that wouldn't stop firing off in her head. She was broken, by her own choice.

She came home and went to bed. She told her mom that she was feeling sick. She slept for a bit and the painful thoughts pulled her out of her sleep. She should have told Jack, but now how could she? It should have been his choice too. What had she done? All of her emotions were conflicted and she was in turmoil.

She had terrible cramps and pain. She looked for the pain pills that she was given. She took one and slept more. She woke again, took another. She woke again and her mind went to the baby she just threw away. She was a terrible person. Jack wouldn't love her anymore. How could he?

The thoughts consumed her every waking moment, and she wondered if the bad thoughts would stop if she took more pills? She clenched that bottle in her hand for hours crying.

She didn't go to school for several days. Her mom checked on her daily.

"Honey, I think you should go to the doctor. I am worried about you."

"I am starting to feel better, Mom," she lied.

Kate came by to check on her and sat on her bed and asked, "What's up with you, Sun, you look like crap?"

Sunny turned to face her and started crying again, pills in hand.

It frightened Kate to see Sunny like this. "Sunny, what is wrong? Should I get your mom?"

"No don't get her, but close the door."

Kate got up and closed the door and said, "Spill it. What's wrong?"

Sunny poured her heart out to Kate, who snuggled in next to her and held her.

"Why didn't you tell me? I would have gone with you." Kate started crying too. "You should not have been alone." She bolted upright. "Why the hell didn't Jack come?"

Sunny started crying again and the look on her face answered her question.

"Oh my God, he doesn't know." She wrapped her arms around her best friend. "Oh, Sunny. Listen to me, we will get through this together. Whether you tell Jack or not, I am here with you."

Kate noticed Sunny's hand and the despair in her eyes, and she gently took her hand and asked, "Can I hold these?"

There was no resistance from her friend.

After a while Sunny physically healed, but she was still emotionally raw. When she spoke with Jack, he believed she was upset about not seeing him all summer, but he still had that uneasy feeling. He was sure it would be better when he saw her next weekend. The distance made him miss her more and he was worried about not seeing her all summer too.

Sunny became withdrawn and depressed. She skipped classes and sat at the beach instead. Sometimes she would go to her and Jack's spot; others to the marina. Sometimes she felt she didn't deserve to see the beautiful water and would just sit in the mall parking lot. She couldn't forgive herself. She couldn't move forward.

It was the weekend Jack was coming and her mom made her a big breakfast. Sunny tried her best to put on her happy face. She hugged her mom and thanked her for breakfast and hugged and kissed her dad. Her parents were worried about her, but they were giving her space to come to them. They never pushed; they trusted Sunny would make the right decisions and come to them when she needed.

The doorbell rang and Sunny opened the door. Jack was such a sight for sore eyes, her heart jumped and broke all at the same time. She put her arms around him whispering his name and breaking down all at the same time.

Jack pulled her back and looked at her face. "Hey, why are you crying? I came here to take my lady out."

He wiped the tears away with his thumbs. Jack thought once he saw her in person his bad feeling would go away, but now it was worse. Sunny pushed Jack out the door and onto the porch. She stood looking into his eyes and knowing that she had to tell him.

"Sunny, you are worrying me, please tell me what's wrong."

"I will. Can we just have this minute?"

She kissed him and all of the guilt, hurt, fear, despair and shame of the past couple of weeks poured out in that kiss. He returned the fervor of the kiss, his fear increasing. Sunny looked into his eyes taking in his every feature.

"Let's take a ride."

"Sure," Jack said, "Where to?"

"Let's go to the marina." Jack knew then that this day was not going to turn out as he had planned.

Sunny told him everything and he sat staring out the window silent. She was waiting for a response from Jack. She was afraid to look at him. The quiet hung in the car like thick fog.

"Jack, say something, please."

"I don't know what to say. You could have called me; I would have come home." Jack said quietly controlling every word. "Why didn't you talk to me, Sunny?"

Sunny winced at the anger in his voice. Jack had never spoken to her like this before. He was quiet again.

Sunny broke the silence, "I know. I am so sorry. I want to go back because I regret everything I have done the past couple of weeks. I was impulsive and scared. I should have talked to you. I hate myself right now and I couldn't bear if you hated me too."

He spoke again without looking her way.

"I don't hate you but I cannot be with you right now. I need to go home."

He started the car and brought Sunny home without another word spoken. He didn't open her door; Jack did not even look at her. Sunny was afraid of this goodbye. Sunny went to her room so quietly her parents didn't hear her come in. She cried again, and this time she couldn't stop. She cried into her pillow, large wracking sobs. He didn't love her anymore. Why couldn't she have just told him when she found out she was pregnant? What was wrong with her? She believed that she was protecting him.

She knew that he would want to marry her, have the baby and figure things out later. They weren't ready for that. He didn't have to give up his plans and dreams because of one mistake that she made. Jack needed to be the architect he wanted to be. He needed to be able to design his dream house. A baby now would have changed all of that. Sunny would not have been able to start college in the fall. It was for the best, the choice she made, but why did it feel so horrible?

Jack was numb by the time he got home. He could not believe what Sunny had done, all alone. Why didn't she talk to him? They told each other everything. What would have happened if she did tell him? Would they have decided to have the baby? He didn't know, because she took that opportunity away. He had never felt so angry. He needed to get away so he could clear his head. He knew what he had to do right now.

He called Sunny. "Hi Mr. Marino, it's Jack. May I speak with Sunny?"

Startled by Jack's voice Gary replied, "Jack, isn't Sunny with you?"

"No, sir, I brought her home earlier."

"Okay, wait and let me see where she is."

As Jack waited he wondered where she could have gone when he heard the rustle of the phone being handled. He heard a barely recognizable *Hello* on the other end.

"Sunny?"

"Yes, Jack, it's me."

"I wanted to let you know I have made a decision; you see that is how this is supposed work. We share important things before we carry them out." Sunny cringed at his words.

"I am going back to school tonight and when I finish my finals I will be going to Italy; I am not coming home before I leave. I think that I need to be far away for a while. I need some time to think and if I come home, my love for you will cloud my judgment."

"Jack, I am more sorry than I can say. But I get it. I won't bother you at all, I will give you the space you need. I love you."

"I know you do. Take care of yourself, Sunny. Goodbye."

Chapter 18

Sunny slid further into herself. Her parents were worried for their daughter. They believed she was suffering from a broken heart. They knew she would come to them when she was ready so they didn't pry. As always they let her know when she needed them they were there. Kate did her best to keep connected with Sunny, but she felt like her friend was slipping away. Sunny told her what happened with Jack. Kate wanted to call him, but she wasn't sure what she would say.

Sunny barely went to any classes anymore, she spent her days wallowing around alone by the bay or walking aimlessly around the mall. Sunny would take any notes that were sent home about her attendance issues out of the mailbox. She would leave and come home at normal times so her parents had no reason to question anything. Sometimes Sunny would go to homeroom to check in and then hang around school.

On one of these days she was sitting outside where the potheads usually were. A girl sat near her giving her the head nod of acknowledgement. She lit up a joint and offered it to Sunny. Sunny hesitated for a minute but took the offered joint. Her first pot experience left her wanting to do it more. She liked how it made her feel, or not feel. Her thoughts of guilt and despair numbed a little and that made her feel better. She hung around with that girl more and smoked pot more often too. Sunny now spent more days at the beach getting high all alone.

After an afternoon of getting high at the beach she made her way home. Her father had gotten home early and got the mail, the letter he opened infuriated him. It was the letter stating her graduation was in jeopardy due to her lack of attendance. He angrily paced waiting for Sunny to get home. He was pissed off at Jack too. He knew the break up was the reason. He should have locked his daughter up long ago. Joann got home before Sunny. Gary had the letter in his hand and started yelling, "Did you know about this?"

"Nice to see you too, dear," she replied calmly and kissed him *hello*, which had a calming effect.

Gary showed her the letter. This was not her Sunshine. The time has come for a serious talk. She was no longer waiting for Sunny to come to her. Sunny came home as usual and went up to her room. Joann convinced Gary to let her try and talk to her first.

She knocked on Sunny's door. "Sunny, it's Mom. Can we talk?"

"Sure, Mom, come in."

Joann went in and sat on her daughter's bed. "Sunny, I have given you space waiting for you to come to me but now I'm asking, what is going on? Have you and Jack broken up?"

"Not exactly, Mom. Jack is leaving for Italy."

"So all of this is because you are going to miss him? I don't buy it because after he came all this way to spend the weekend with you, he left the same day. What happened?"

Sunny's eyes started to fill up and she knew the crying wasn't far behind. She was stuck. She was not accustomed to lying to her mother but how could she tell her what a terrible person she was? Maybe her mother wouldn't love her anymore either and would want to leave her too.

"He needed some space and distance, so he is leaving for Italy without coming home to say goodbye."

"I am sorry to hear that but, Sunny, there's another problem. You are not going to graduate. We received notice from school today. I know you are upset, but you have to put school first."

"Mom, I just can't bear to be in class. I can't concentrate, I don't listen."

"That's not acceptable. You have college in the fall. How can you do that if you don't finish high school? You need to pick yourself up by your bootstraps and get to class. I am here if you need to talk about Jack or how upset you are. I can understand that, but I cannot understand or tolerate you skipping school. Pull yourself together, Sunshine."

Sunny couldn't even imagine *pulling herself together.* All she could think of was getting high and making these feelings go away.

"I'll try, Mom." Joann didn't believe her daughter for the first time in her seventeen years.

Joann had a feeling this was more than a break up and she was torn between holding her daughter and begging her to tell her what was wrong or trying some tough love. She went with the latter because she was also fairly certain that her daughter was high. Joann thought her daughter needed a wake-up call.

"Listen, Sunny, either you get it together and get back to class or you have to get a full-time job. We don't sit around here doing nothing. You will get over Jack and when you do, you will want to go to college and become the best nurse you can be."

As she said the words she realized her daughter was going to Jack's college. She should have held her and tried getting her to talk.

"Sunny, please, if there is anything you want to talk about, I am always here to listen. I love you and you are worrying me."

"I know, Mom. I can't talk about it right now, but maybe one day I will." Her mom let it go for the time being, but she had a feeling this was far from over.

Joann filled Gary in on their talk and her feelings that there was more to the story. But Sunny wasn't ready to talk about it. She also told him she thought their daughter was high. Gary was wanted to run up to her room and shake her back to her senses. He had a tendency to react and sweep up the mess later, with teenage girls that did not work, so he usually let Joann lead the way. He trusted his wife's judgment. She was always so good at this stuff. It was one of the reasons they made a good team. He just hoped the choices his daughter was making now didn't impact her future.

Unfortunately that was not the case. Sunny didn't graduate. While Kate was going to the prom they planned, Sunny spent more time alone, getting high. All the preparations they made for their senior year and Kate was without her best friend. Kate wanted to help, but she had no idea of what to do. She kept coming by, calling, but Sunny was barely responsive.

Sunny lost her desire to go to college, especially the school where Jack was. He didn't want to see her, and she didn't blame him. She preferred not to see herself. She hurt him; she hurt their baby; she didn't deserve him. She ruined everything. Who would want to be with her?

Sunny slipped further away. Gary and Joann tried to reach out to her, but Sunny kept herself closed off. The day Mr. Muncey called to offer her some summer hours it gave them hope, she loved that job. When Sunny spoke with him she declined the offer. That was a nice, happy job and she didn't deserve that.

Joann felt Sunny needed do something. If she was not going to school then she had to work. Sunny reluctantly agreed.

She found a job on Fire Island, but not in Ocean Beach. She started working as a waitress in one of the two restaurants in Kismet. She needed things to be different. She wanted to be anywhere but her hometown or any place familiar. Her beloved town no longer gave her the comfort she was accustomed to. Now it made her want to crawl under a rock. When people looked in her direction she thought they knew what she had done. She needed anonymity. When she filled out her application at the restaurant she got the idea to use her middle name. As Rey, she could be someone else here. She liked that. She could stop being Sunshine. She left Sunshine in Seaville.

Rey started working on the weekends in June. Businesses didn't really get crazy busy until Fourth of July weekend. She met some new people at work and they all shared a house for the season. There was one share left in their house and she took it. It was one of three twin beds in a small room. When she told her parents they were devastated. Deep down they knew Sunny had to work this out so they agreed, hoping that she would come out of this depression and get her life back on track. Kate was broken hearted too. She'd thought they would work together one last time and get ready for college. She had been so worried about her friend and thought the summer would bring them back together.

No one could reach Sunny, not her mom, dad or Kate. They were at a loss of how to bring her back. So they did the only thing they could, they let her go.

Chapter 19

Jack hugged and kissed his parents and Hannah goodbye at John F. Kennedy International Airport. He was nervous to be going to another country where he did not speak the language, all alone. He was apprehensive and excited about this experience but there was one thing missing from this bon voyage, Sunny. He felt if he knew Sunny was here, supporting him he might feel more self-assured. He was still mad, but part of him was hoping she would show up here at the airport. He lingered a few extra minutes but she never showed. He knew he needed to get on the plane. Jack needed to put all his attention into this internship. Impulsively he also signed up for the following semester's classes in Italy.

He arrived in Italy and the representative from Alaimo and Associates International, Gianni was there to greet him. Thankfully he spoke English. Jack had been studying Italian since he accepted the offer, but he was not confident in his language acquisitions skills yet. All of his living arrangements were made by AA, Int., so there were no worries there. Gianni took him to his apartment. Jack sat with his face pressed against the window, in awe. It was everything he envisioned and so much more.

The internship was off to a great start. Many people spoke English and his Italian improved. He took several tours during his off times and the countryside was just amazing. Jack sat on a bus that rode up and down the hills ogling the lemon groves, olive trees and grapes growing. He would sit in a piazza for hours just looking at the architecture around him. He loved to scrutinize every line in a column leading up to the carved angels at the top. He felt as though he would never tire of studying these magnificent structures. Jack found himself thinking of how he couldn't wait to share this with Sunny. He wanted to call her and tell her everything, but he didn't. He made a promise to himself to focus on his work and not let his love trouble interfere, but it did anyway.

He didn't know if he could forgive Sunny. He was no longer mad about what she did. Given the opportunity they may have come to the same decision together. What angered him so much was that she did not give him that option. She completely cut him out. It was his baby too.

The vision that haunted him was the look of pain on her face. At the time he was so mad he didn't care. The only thing he needed in that moment was to not look into her face. That was the look he saw every night when he closed his eyes. One night while he was lying in bed trying to shake it from his memory, it hit him. Sunny had tried to tell him the night he told her about Italy. He went over and over that conversation in his mind. She protected him. He knew how her mind worked.

It was a turning point for Jack. He started to feel as if he might be able to forgive Sunny and his heart started to open a tiny bit. He was still deeply hurt that she did not come to him and talk about it. He wanted desperately to discuss this with her, so she could help him understand. The distance was killing him.

They left things so unsettled. He thought distance was what he needed. They should have talked after the initial anger and hurt he felt.

He spent sleepless nights going over everything. So many regrets, the more he thought about the whole situation, the more he believed that he would have come to the same decision to terminate the pregnancy. When he realized that, he knew he had to call Sunny.

He was trying to figure out the best time. He thought about her and where she was at this moment. She might be on Fire Island with her family. It was the end of July. He missed her birthday and hoped she had a good day.

The next day he said out loud. "Forget it, there is no right time." He picked up the phone in his apartment and started putting in all the necessary numbers to make an international call. It was 11:00 pm in Italy, which meant it was 5:00 pm on Long Island. Mr. Marino answered the phone.

"Hello, Mr. Marino, this is Jack, how are you doing?"

"Fine, Jack. What can I do for you?" Mr. Marino was curt.

"I would like to speak with Sunny."

Gary took a breath in. He really wanted to let Jack have it after all the trouble he has caused his little girl, but instead he said through tight lips, "Sunny is not here."

"Do you know when she will be in?"

Jack asked, suddenly feeling uncomfortable. Mr. Marino sounded angry and he wasn't sure why.

"Sometime after Labor Day," he replied and hung up.

Jack couldn't believe what he just heard. Where the hell was Sunny and what happened? He tried calling Kate, but there was no answer at her house. He didn't know what to do being so far away. There was nothing he could do but work his butt off and get back home to find Sunny. And so that's what he did.

Sunny spent her eighteenth birthday with her coworkers. They celebrated by drinking tequila. After lots of tequila, Sunny went down by the dock alone. She got high and watched the sun come up. She continued to party like that almost every night. Sunny spent her days at the beach nursing her hangover, evenings working and nights drinking and smoking pot. She would make her way back to the house she shared with her coworkers, to her thin, lumpy bed and pass out only to repeat the process the next day.

One particularly lonely night, she was sitting on the dock holding her Walkman in one hand and a joint in another. She listened to *You're My Best Friend*, the lyrics stabbed her in her soul and she started crying uncontrollably. She couldn't take feeling like this so she walked back to her room and grabbed a bottle of vodka she kept under her bed. She went down to the ocean and drank until she no longer remembered her name. The morning sun on her sand covered face woke her. She got up and threw her Walkman into the ocean with the Queen cassette still in it.

Kate came to visit Sunny and she looked happy to see her. She asked her to hang out until after her shift so they could go next door.

Kate said, "I thought we could go sit on the beach and star gaze and talk for a while."

"Wouldn't you rather have a shot of tequila? The stars will look much better then." Kate did not want one but thought it might be the only way to get her to agree.

"Okay, Sunny, one shot and then the beach."

Sunny kept her word to her friend and as they sat on the beach side by side, Sunny leaned into Kate and let the tears roll.

"I hate the way I feel Kate. When I don't drink or get high, I think too much about everything and I feel like my heart is ripped into pieces." Kate put her arms around her friend trying to figure out how she could help.

"Why don't you come home, Sunny? We will figure out how to make you feel better."

"You can't. I am not worth the effort. I threw my baby away and I didn't even tell Jack. He was so disgusted that he left without saying goodbye and I don't blame him." She was sobbing now. "It feels like there's darkness inside me that only brightens when I drink or smoke."

Kate was scared for her friend. She thought carefully about what she said next. She was afraid Sunny would fall further away if it came out wrong.

"Sunny, listen, you didn't throw your baby away. You made a difficult choice, and now you are having regrets and your heart is broken. You aren't thinking clearly, you drink too much, you get high too much, and you dropped out of school. You are letting your life fall apart because you regret a choice you made. Jack is an asshole for not saying goodbye. You deserved that much. Let me help you figure out a way to get past this. Come home and see your parents. They are worried about you."

Sunny reluctantly agreed to visit home for a couple of days, she switched her shifts with someone else so she could have two consecutive days off and she headed back with Kate the next morning.

Chapter 20

Gary and Joann were thrilled to see Sunny. They tried to mask the pain in their eyes when they got a good look at their daughter.

"You have lost weight, sweetheart. Are you eating enough?" Joann said over the lump in her throat.

"Mom made your favorite, chicken cutlets with her famous macaroni and cheese."

Gary managed to sound cheerful. At least tonight she would have a good meal. They ate and made small talk. Gary decided he wasn't going to tell Sunny about Jack's call, she looked bad enough. If Jack were here right now, he would strangle him.

Gary went out and got ice cream after dinner. The three of them sat on the porch and ate their ice cream.

"Tell me about your job, Sunshine."

Sunny didn't look up. "It's okay."

Joann tried. "How are the people in the house?"

"Fine."

Her parents continued to try and pry conversation from their daughter to no avail. Sunny said goodnight and went to bed. Gary and Joann discussed Sunny and what they could do about her.

"She looks terrible and I feel so helpless. I am not even sure if this is all about the breakup." Joann was tearing up as she spoke.

"I don't have the answer either. Do we make her stay here or let her work this out on her own?" He was running his hands through his hair in frustration. "You usually have insight that I don't when it comes to our little girl but this is killing me seeing her like this." Gary was choking up as well.

"I am going to try and get her to talk to me, Gary. It's all I have." Joann got up and headed upstairs.

"Sunny, can I come in?"

"Sure, Mom. I'm just lying here."

"Sunny, Daddy and I are worried about you. You look like you have been to hell and back. Is it all because of Jack? Did you two break up before he left?"

Sunny took a long breath in and let it out slowly. "That is part of it, Mom. We didn't actually break up, but Jack couldn't stand to be with me anymore."

"What the hell does that mean?" Joann's voice rose.

"I did something terrible and did not tell him."

"Another boy and he found out?"

"I wish, Mom. No, it is much worse than that." The tears started to well up in her eyes.

"Sunny, what could you have possibly done? You are a wonderful girl with no malice in your heart."

Sunny looked at her mom and back down at her hands wishing there was a shot of tequila in them right now. She took a deep breath and decided to tell her mother what an awful person she was. She spoke in a barely audible whisper.

"I had an abortion and told him after."

Joann was stupefied. She took a minute to process what her daughter had just told her. She took her for birth control pills. She did all the right things to prevent this. She had lots of questions but she needed to gather her wits. Joann was fighting back tears.

"When?

What about your pills?

Why didn't you come to me?

Did Kate go with you?"

Sunny shook her head as her mother fired off each question. A look of horror crawled across Joann's face as she realized Sunny had been alone and she could no longer keep the tears at bay. Joann took her daughter in her arms and the warmth of her mother's touch was Sunny's undoing. As they held each other and cried Joann murmured into her ear.

"I am so sorry you did that alone, my baby. Oh, Sunny." She whispered it over and over again.

She understood Sunny's despair. Sunny left no detail out when she was able to speak.

"Look at me, Sunny. You did nothing wrong. You made a choice; a choice woman didn't always have. It is your body."

"I was so scared, Mom, but I felt I made the right choice at the time."

"You were fortunate to be able to go to a medical facility with trained personnel. You live in a time when it is your right to choose, don't be ashamed of that."

"I am ashamed of everything, most of all how I treated Jack."

"My only question is why you chose to keep it from him. This is not a judgment in any way I was wondering what drove that decision. You two were so close and anyone can see you had a special connection."

Sunny explained it all. "I just made the decision and did it very quickly, but when I was lying there I was so scared. I felt so isolated. I know it was my choice to do it alone, but as it happened I realized the ramifications of what I was doing."

Once the floodgates opened Sunny couldn't stop. She told her mom everything including the feelings she was having about God being mad at her, worrying about having children when the time was right.

Joann started crying again. "No wonder you feel so lost, my love, but please don't shut us out anymore. We all love you and want to help you through this."

Sunny nodded in agreement and her mom assumed she would come back home, but she said she was going to finish out the season in Kismet. She said the change of scenery was good for her. She still needed space. She wasn't ready to be Sunshine again. It felt good to tell her mother everything. She felt slightly lighter and her heart didn't hurt as much.

She spent the next day with Kate who noticed a difference in her friend. Sunny told her that she shared everything with her mom. She was also relieved that she saw a glimpse of her old friend Sunny. They had a great day together just being girls again. Kate was so excited about school and was going on and on about her classes when she stopped and looked at Sunny.

"I'm sorry. Does it bother you?"

"What? Not going to school in the fall? I haven't even thought about it yet. Please don't let that stop you I am happy for you so don't leave anything out."

It felt so good, being with each other again. At least one of the stars in the galaxy was back where it belonged.

Chapter 21

Sunny went back to Kismet and tried to move forward. She tried to not drink and smoke every night. During her shift one Saturday night she glanced toward the bar and her heart skipped a beat. She pushed her way through the crowd toward the man, he turned around. It was not Jack. She could feel the tears slide down her face. As soon as she got off work, she headed next door.

"Gimme two shots of whatever is in your hand, Tom. I need to forget today."

"You got it, Rey." He poured both shots into one glass and placed it in front of her.

Tom refilled her glass over and over until closing time.

"Rey, want me to walk you home?" Tom offered.

"No. Thanks." She slurred each word. Sunny slid off the barstool and made her way to the door.

Sunny weaved her way through the sidewalks when Tom came up behind her. He wound his arm around her waist.

"I got you, Rey, now let's get you home." He started running his hand down to her bottom and gave it a squeeze. He stopped in the street to pull her toward him. He pressed his groin against her.

"C'mon let me help you forget today too."

It took Sunny a minute to comprehend what was going on. In her drunken state she was awkwardly pushing him away.

"I only want Jack, you're not him."

"You can call me whatever you want." He held her tighter.

Sunny was trying to squirm free and started to panic. She started to cry. Tom let go and the force of her trying to get free knocked her to the ground.

"You are a basket case, Rey; I don't need this shit." He left her crying on the ground.

Sunny had no idea how long she was lying there when her coworker and housemate Paul, came along. He rushed to her side and helped her up. She was a mess. Her head was bleeding, her makeup was smeared all over her swollen face and her clothes were muddy.

"What the hell happened, Rey?"

"Tom from the out decided to walk me home and was mad that I didn't want to thank him." She was still slurring her words.

"Piece of shit." He mumbled taking her hand and guiding her home.

Paul helped her inside and cleaned her up. He gently dabbed at her cut with a paper towel, he pushed her hair back from her face. He wet the paper towel and cleaned her makeup too.

"Rey, you need to stop drinking, you are going to get hurt. There are lots of assholes like Tom around that are just waiting to take advantage."

"You may be right. I was really frightened by him tonight." Sunny shuddered at what could have happened.

"Tomorrow morning you and I will have a real talk about this. Now you are going to go to bed." He kissed her on her head and said goodnight.

The next morning she had an enormous hangover. She brushed her teeth three times and still didn't feel clean. She made her way into the kitchen and Paul was already up and having coffee.

"Good morning, Sunshine." Sunny's head jerked toward Paul.

"What?" Sunny couldn't believe her ears.

"Jeez Rey, good morning, Sunshine; it's something people say to one another. Would you rather good morning, idiot?" Paul was smiling wide.

Relieved, Sunny smiled back. "No it was nice to hear."

"You hung over?"

"Yes and it's a whopper, I think I might throw up."

"I have the perfect cure. Follow me."

He grabbed her hand and they headed to the beach. He never let go of her hand until they dove under a wave.

"Best cure ever."

Sunny agreed. They sat on the beach for a while discussing the events of the previous night.

"Thank you, Paul. If you hadn't come along I'd still be lying out there."

"I am glad you are okay, but I was serious last night. You need to be more careful. You get so drunk and walked around alone. It's dangerous." Paul was genuinely concerned for her.

"You are right. I am not going to let that happen again. It is time I got my shit together."

Sunny put her energy into work. It felt good to keep busy all the time. She would work whenever anyone asked her to. It helped to keep the darkness in her at bay. One slow day at work she was chatting with Paul.

"Rey, where do you work off season?"

"I don't have anything lined up so I am not sure where I will work when the season is over."

"I work in a restaurant in Manhattan. The money is good, not like Fire Island summer good, but pretty close. We are always looking for hard workers like you. What do you think, Rey?" asked Paul.

"I'll think about it and let you know. I would have to find a place to live blah, blah, blah," Sunny said smiling.

Paul said, "Okay but I'll put in the good word for you if you want it."

As time went by the bad thoughts stopped consuming her. They lingered in a blurred place in the back of her mind. The thought of Jack no longer made her wince. The pain still lived within her; it just wasn't right there on the surface ready to implode. She was able to manage a real smile or two these days. Time heals all wounds. Her mom had told her that so it must be true.

The season's end was approaching and she wasn't quite sure what she wanted to do. Sunny was the only one left in the share house, as she had paid through the end of September. All of the other occupants had already left for school and the real world. It left her with an abundance of time to think. She knew that she couldn't go on the way she was, working, getting high, drinking, escaping repeat. She decided it was time to pick herself up by her bootstraps. Her mom would be proud of the euphemism. It's just that she wasn't sure what to do once she stood on her feet.

Nursing school, especially at Jack's school, was out of the question. Not just because of Jack, either. She hadn't even graduated high school. The thought of Jack made her sad. She truly ruined everything and clearly he was done with her. Sunny didn't even blame him. She knew it was her fault, that she had broken them apart.

If she was going to attempt to get herself back together she knew what her first step would be. She made an appointment to get her GED. She wasn't sure if wanted to be a nurse anymore but before she could consider any career she needed a high school diploma.

Until she was ready to make any type of career decisions she was going to take the Manhattan restaurant job. She came to that decision when Paul told her that his friend needed to sublet his apartment and offered it to her. Sunny went to see it. It was on the Lower East Side in a not so nice neighborhood and it was tiny. But it was a fresh start, a new beginning.

She needed to be independent so she could figure out what path she would go down. She felt satisfied with her decision to live and work in Manhattan. She couldn't believe that she was going to live in the city. She had never entertained the thought. Her next step, break the news to her parents.

Chapter 22

Sunny hopped the last ferry for the evening and came home for a couple of days. She wanted to spend the day with Kate and find out how college was. She also knew she had to speak with her parents.

While Sunny was out to lunch with Kate, her friend said, "Holy shit I almost forgot. Remember Psychic Mike?"

Sunny started laughing, "Psychic Sundays Psychic Mike?"

"The one and only," Kate said.

"What about him?" Sunny asked.

"I got an appointment for a private reading. Someone at school had it but could not keep the appointment. There's a yearlong wait list so I took the appointment with him and I can bring a friend, want to go?"

Sunny thought she had nothing to lose, maybe he could tell her what to do with her life. Plus it would give her another day with Kate.

"Why not? That sounds cool. When is it?"

"Tomorrow, I thought I would surprise you. I know the first question I will ask him will be how wonderful I am going to do in school…oh, I mean college. I am a very important college girl now so please remember that when you speak with me." She broke out in laughter and Sunny couldn't help but join her. She forgot how good it felt to laugh with her friend Kate. Sunny told her parents where she and Kate were going the next day.

"Yes, I seem to remember you two listening to his radio show, I am sure it will be good for a laugh." Gary was fiddling with his stereo as he spoke.

"A few months ago I would have said the same thing until I called in one night and he told me stuff about Papa that no one else knew, not even you or mommy."

Sunny rehashed the call and she wished she remembered everything Psychic Mike told her before she made the choices she did and threw her life into turmoil. Her grandpa was right. She needed to rely on those who love her. She made a decision right then to do just that.

The next afternoon Sunny and Kate arrived at Psychic Mike's home which Sunny thought odd. She had expected an office, like a counselor, but he had a special reading room in his house. Mike was very welcoming as if they were friends coming for a visit. He had a nervous energy about him. Kate went first. Sunny stayed quietly in the living room looking around. On the end table sat a statue of the Blessed Mother. A picture of Jesus hung from the wall over the couch. On the opposite wall was a wooden, hand carved cross. He was most definitely a religious man. It took her by surprise. Wasn't Mike's profession thought to be sacrilege? Maybe her perception of what he did was wrong.

Kate and Sunny each had tape recorders, Mike encouraged all his clients to bring one. Sunny sat patiently for an hour before Kate emerged. Sunny tried to read her face but her own apprehension clouded her vision.

It was Sunny's turn. She almost dropped her tape recorder, she caught it before it hit the floor. She followed with shaky legs. The reading room was dark with a wooden dresser along one wall with more religious statues and pictures. There were two chairs that faced one another right in the center of the room. The furniture was dark wood. Sunny felt so safe. As she sat in the chair a feeling passed through her. The only way she could describe it was it felt like the presence of God.

The reading began: Mike held a pile of construction paper in his lap, and he furiously scribbled on the top page. He explained that he channeled his surges of energy from the *other side* and the scribbling helped him to relieve the energy for a clear message. He started giving her names and asking if they had meaning to her. Some she recognized and some she didn't. Then he said, "The male figure here is your grandfather and he is saying you did not listen to his advice." Sunny was momentarily perplexed but then connected it to the night she called into the radio show.

"Your grandfather warned you of a challenge and that you should lean on the people who love you."

Sunny nodded knowing he was right. The scribbling increased and Mike looked directly in Sunny's eyes.

"You have lost a child?"

She shook her head *no*. In her mind she did not lose a child, she threw it away.

"No, you lost a child. You had an abortion."

The blood drained from her head and rested on her shoulders as the weight that had slowly lifted over these past few months came back all at once.

"This is not meant to make you feel bad or be some kind of guilt trip. Your baby is fine. In fact, he is with your grandfather. He knew that the time wasn't right for him and when the time is right he will come back. He is waiting in heaven for that time."

So that's what her grandfather meant, she thought. She should have counted on those she loves and who love her. Sunny was no longer sure if Mike was still talking; she could not hear over the sound of her burden lifting away. Her heart felt lighter too. If her son was waiting in heaven, or the other side, to be hers, God couldn't be possibly be angry.

Chapter 23

Sunny sat with her parents that evening sharing her reading as well as her plans. They noticed the change in her demeanor. Whether or not they believed it seemed to make Sunny feel better. Gary spoke first.

"Sunny, I know you have been to hell and back these last few months and I would have done anything to take some of your hurt. I am proud of who you are and support you now and always."

"Daddy, thank you. I am sorry if I disappointed you. I felt like a terrible person."

"You are a wonderful person," Joann and Gary said in unison.

"It is okay for you to move forward now, Sunshine. We are not crazy about you living in the city all by yourself but we will come in to visit a lot." Joann took Sunny's hand as she spoke, "Please remember that if you start feeling down you can call us anytime. We will be a train ride away. Promise you won't slip away from us again."

"I am going to try my best to make a fresh start. I am going to start my new job soon. I will work in Kismet until the end of the month and I will have a week to move and

settle in before I start work in Manhattan." Sunny seemed
satisfied.

Chapter 24

December, 1982.

Jack returned from Italy. He knew he would miss so many things about Italy. He missed the history that surrounded him everywhere he went. He missed the way everyone rested in the middle of the day and spent time with family. But what he missed most was sharing it with Sunny. He knew what he had to do. He needed to see Sunny before they just bumped into each other on campus. He wanted to make things right. He mustered up all of his humility and went to Sunny's house. He knocked on the door and was relieved when Joann answered it. After his conversation with Gary months ago, he was a little intimidated by him.

"Hi, Mrs. Marino. It's nice to see you. Is Sunny around?" Joann held the door open and stepped back indicating to him to come in.

"Have a seat, Jack."

She motioned to the kitchen table, the very table he was sitting at the first time he met her. It was the same day he knew he was crazy about Sunny. Joann started with some pleasantries asking about his internship and how he liked living in another country. Jack was enthusiastic talking about his experience but he was wondering where Sunny was.

"Sunny is not here, Jack," she answered his question before he asked.

"Will she be back soon?"

"No she won't. As a matter of fact she will not be coming back at all, she has moved out."

Joann knew that this was not entirely true, but she wanted to make Jack squirm. She wanted him to ask for an explanation. Jack was stunned. He never expected to hear that. Suddenly his throat felt like it was closing.

"Where did she move to?"

"The city."

Joann said curtly not offering other details. She was going to make him sweat this out.

"As in New York City? How did that come about? Is she going to school there now?" Jack had fifty more questions but he was trying very hard not to panic.

"Well, Jack, do you want to know what happened to my daughter, really?"

"Yes, Mrs. Marino I want to know everything. I had time to do a lot of thinking, I have made mistakes and I want to make things right with her, I love her."

"*I know,* Jack," but the way she emphasized her words made him realize that she didn't mean him loving her.

She knew about the pregnancy, but then again of course she would, Sunny told her everything. Jack's shoulders dropped and he sat back in his chair unsure if he was really ready to hear what she was going to say.

Joann began, "I see you know what I mean. Sunny went through the ordeal for the most part, alone." She held her hand in the air and continued. "She chose not to tell you and that was a mistake, I agree. It was a split-second decision she made in a very emotional state thinking it was the right one. She loved you so much and thought she was protecting your dreams and in doing that, she lost her own. You left her to deal with the aftermath alone. You didn't even say goodbye and that made her think she wasn't worthy of your time."

Jack studied Joann's face as she spoke, intently listening to every word. He started to speak.

"That was not my intention, I was so upset myself I couldn't think clearly. I can never think clearly when she is with me," Jack barely whispered.

"I can understand that, Jack. But I am telling you Sunny's story right now. It's what you want to know, right?"

He nodded acknowledgment. "You're right, I do."

"Sunny started to hate herself. She couldn't cope with the guilt and your rejection. She withdrew from everything. She thought getting high and drinking was the best way to deal with her feelings. Sunny didn't graduate high school and won't be attending college."

Jack could feel his heart breaking into pieces.

"She went to Fire Island to work this summer." Jack imagined her working in the ice cream shop and knew how much she enjoyed it, and he smiled.

"…not in Ocean Beach, but Kismet. Every night she would stumble into her lonely little bed in a house full of strangers. She shut all of us out and was destroying herself."

Jack stifled a sob. He was jumping out of his skin knowing what happened, if her face haunted him while he was away thinking she was home safe, he couldn't imagine what everyone went through seeing Sunny like this. He fought the urge to run out the door and find Sunny right now. He was responsible for this. Why didn't he just talk to her before he left? He needed to hear everything so he stayed. He hung his head.

"Please tell me the rest."

"Kate was the one that finally got through to her and convinced her to come home for a visit. It was during that visit she told us the whole story. All this time we'd thought it was just the break up that she couldn't cope with, and I was angry that she was so upset over losing you. When I found out everything that had happened I became mad at myself for not being with her through everything. She promised me that she wouldn't withdraw anymore. Finally little glimpses of her started to show. Her heart is healing and she is moving forward. She has had to struggle to claw her way out of the darkness she put herself in, and she is still fragile. She got a job and an apartment in Manhattan, and she says it's her new beginning."

Jack sat for a couple of minutes letting all that had happened to Sunny sink in.

"I can't begin to tell you how sorry I am for my part in all of this, I was so upset myself that I didn't realize what Sunny may have been going through. I was so far away so it was easy to believe things were the same here. I would do anything to take it all back. I love Sunny."

"I am sure you do, Jack. But I am going to ask you a big favor. Leave her alone right now. She is too fragile still. I am afraid if she heads down that destructive path again we might not get her back. She just started smiling again. If you really love her, go back to school and be the best you can be. That's why she made the choices she did. Be worthy of that Jack."

He rose and as he did he felt his heart crushing inside his chest. He could not hurt Sunny again. He wanted nothing more than to run and find her, stroke her hair and run kisses all over her face. The last thing he ever wanted would be to cause her more heartache.

"Okay, Mrs. Marino. I will leave her alone; I won't be the cause of anymore hurt." He stood with the weight of what he just learned on his shoulders.

As he was turning to head out the door, Joann said, "Jack, look at me." She held him on both of his arms looking at him. "You are a good man, Jack. Circumstances got out of control, but my Sunshine would not have loved you so much if you were not a kind person."

She saw the tears welling in his eyes. Everyone has been hurt enough. She hugged him and he let her.

Chapter 25

Jack went back to school and did as he promised. He worked and studied all the time. He was able to graduate in December, 1983, a full semester early and with honors. His hard work didn't go unnoticed, either. He had a job offer right out of school. Alaimo and Associates valued his work in Italy and hired him as an associate. He often thought of Sunny and if she was okay, but he would not break his promise to her mom or to himself. Sunny worked hard not to think about Jack. And enough time had passed that only occasionally, Jack emerged from the back of her mind and it didn't hurt like it used to.

She couldn't believe that she lived and worked in Manhattan for more than a year already. Sunny was confident that she made the right decision to move here. She felt independent and liked discovering herself. She really liked her job. The people were fun to work with and she made lots of money. The restaurant was near Wall Street and the patrons were mostly business people. Sunny continued using her middle name at work. That was how Paul knew her and it was just easier to keep it that way. Her name tag read, *Rey* and it was always a conversation starter.

People usually asked what it was short for or if her parents wanted a boy.

The lunch shift was the busiest and Sunny never minded working a double shift. Her apartment suited her needs, it was tiny and tidy and all hers. Her parents bought her all kinds of things for her apartment and helped her set it up. The biggest purchase was a pull-out couch, so they always had a place to stay. That suited Sunny just fine.

Kate came to visit at the end of the semester and stayed for the weekend. Sunny had really missed her friend who was so happy because she met her *one true love,* her words. Kate in love was so much fun to be around. Sunny wondered if she had been the same way.

"Sunny, I love going to school. Education is definitely my thing."

"Good thing since you are going to be a teacher." Sunny brightly smiled.

Kate started to giggle. "Ask me my boyfriend's name."

Sunny played along. "Okay…what is this man's name?"

"Nate!" Kate blurted out. The two could not stop laughing.

"Really, Kate and Nate? That is way too much." Sunny hugged her friend. "I am so thrilled you found your *one.*"

They talked just like old times and Kate felt it, her friend was truly back and she couldn't be happier.

"Sunny, I can't believe I'm in my second year of college, it went so fast and you have lived in the big city for over a year now. It is almost like we are growing up, imagine that."

Sunny came home for her parents annual Christmas Eve Soiree. Kate and Nate were there too and it was evident they loved each other immensely. Sunny thought Nate was great but she couldn't stand all the rhyming! Sunny couldn't remember the last time she enjoyed herself this much. Neither did Joann or Gary. Everyone told stories, sang songs and laughed until the wee hours. Sunny felt at home again.

The next morning Sunny got up early and sat by the Christmas tree alone. She sipped her morning coffee which she began drinking recently, and for the first time in a very long time felt happy. She had made some decisions and couldn't wait to share them with her parents. Gary and Joann came downstairs. Gary kissed her on her head and wished her a Merry Christmas.

"Merry Christmas, Daddy." He loved the way it felt when she called him daddy. Her mom brought in two more cups of coffee and handed one to her dad.

"Merry Christmas, Sunshine."

Sunny looked at both of her parents. "Mom, Dad, I have been doing a lot of thinking about what I want to do with my life. I know that I do not want to be a nurse anymore."

"You know you can be whatever you want, love." Joann said.

"I think I want to be a counselor. I want to help troubled teens like me. Who better to counsel someone than a person who has been through troubles too! I am going to start taking some classes this spring."

"Is there still time to sign up for classes?" Gary asked.

"What about your GED?" Joann asked.

"I already got my GED and I signed up for classes too." Sunny said proudly. "I know it's going to be hard, but I have worked it out with work and they will schedule me around my classes. This is going to be good for me."

Joann and Gary were thrilled. This was the best present they could have asked for.

There she was, their levelheaded, mature daughter was back with them this Christmas Day. They told her not to worry about the cost because they had saved for her education. She started her classes in January, 1984.

Living their own separate lives they embarked on new journeys without each other. In the back of their respective minds was their love.

Jack gave his career one hundred and ten percent and he was well respected and liked. He kept his focus on his job and couldn't believe he had been working at AA and Associates for one year already. He was lonely. He missed sharing himself, he dated a bit but no one had really held his interest. He dated one girl for about two months and she wanted more from him than he had to give. They stopped seeing each other and Jack didn't even seem to notice. Sunny was still in his heart. Jack would catch a glimpse of an ice cream cone, hear a song or gaze up at the night sky and he would see Sunny's face. Jack made a long-term plan, he wanted to open his own firm one day and he kept that goal in mind every day at work.

Sunny enjoyed her classes. The first semester she took just a couple of classes and liked it so much she took more the next semester. She still worked at the restaurant but she liked being busy. She also liked walking around the city where not one person recognized who you were, a feeling she never thought she'd enjoy.

One of the things she'd always loved about her hometown was that everyone knew everyone, but at this time in her life she needed to be anonymous. She needed to by *Rey*. She dated Paul on and off during this time. He was really nice and she enjoyed his company, but mostly she liked the friendship. He also didn't know Sunshine, he knew Rey. And they were very different. She liked it that way.

During one of her visits home, she was talking with her mom discussing school and her job when her mom told her about Jack's visit when he got home from Italy. Joann felt her daughter was in a place where she could hear it without being devastated or drop everything and run to him.

Gary walked into the room. Sunny looked up at him. "You knew too?"

"Yes, sweetheart, but you need to understand that we felt we were so close to losing you and you were just starting to emerge from your depression we didn't want to risk it. We wanted Jack to know how he hurt you too. But we don't hate him. As matter of fact your mom told him as much."

Tears pooled in his eyes as he spoke. Sunny finally understood how her actions impacted her parents. She had put them through hell and she made a promise to herself that she would never do that to them again. She hugged them both. Everyone's tears flowed freely.

"I get it, and it's okay. You are probably right; I would have run to him and stopped all the things I am doing now. I guess you guys are smarter than I thought." The tears turned to laughter.

The following summer, 1985, some of the staff at the restaurant went to Fire Island to work, including Paul. Sunny stayed to take a few summer classes. She was glad to have a break from Paul. He was starting to want more of a relationship than she was willing to give.

It was a beautiful day and Sunny walked to work. She was just working the lunch shift today and planned on going to the park later to enjoy the weather. When she arrived she saw all the staff on shift today had been trained by her. Sunny was confident they would be able to handle the rush. She went about her daily tasks and before long the customers starting pouring in.

She was thankful for her crew because they were slammed during their shift and they handled it beautifully. They were running from table to table taking orders, bussing, and cleaning like a well-oiled machine, Sunny loved these types of days, they went by fast, she made lots of money and it was fun. Sunny had what she called her *waitress smile*. It was the fake *sure I'd love to get you 20 things one at a time* smiles. The smile only incorporated her mouth, it never reached her eyes to make them twinkle, but no one noticed. It was her little joke she shared with everyone she trained. She told them as long as the customer believes you live to wait on them your tips will reflect that. She headed over to a new table, a party of eight, with her best waitress smile.

"Good afternoon everyone. My name is Rey and I will be taking good care of you today. Who would like to start with a cocktail?"

Sunny started looking to each patron for their drink order. There were actually six men and two women, and one of the men had his arm draped across the back of the chair next to him. As Sunny's eyes reached that man's face she froze. It was a profile she knew as well as her own face. She was rooted to her spot trying to gain her words back. She felt dizzy and thought she might collapse, but she took a deep, steadying breath, put on her best waitress smile and asked, "What would you like to drink, Jack?" All the while pleading with herself, don't fall, keep your feet planted, breathe in, breathe out.

Hearing his name he turned his body away from the woman and looked up, stunned. Could it be, his Sunshine right here at his table? He wanted to jump up and throw his arms around her. He was with his coworkers and a potential client so he needed to remain calm and professional, but he wanted to scream her name.

"How are you? You look wonderful."

She kept her exterior composure. "Thank you. I'm fine. What would you like to drink?"

He asked for water and studied her as she took the remainder of the orders. He was the only one at the table that could read her face, that smile didn't even come close to a Sunny smile. He was trying to figure out a way to excuse himself to talk with Sunny. His boss started to engage him in conversation, but he had no idea what the man had said. The only thing he knew was that this was his chance. It was a sign, and he needed to talk to her. A coworker's voice brought him back to the present.

"You seemed to know our waitress, who is she?"

"She was my first love." His answer seemed to satisfy his coworkers and one of them gave a wink and said, "Nothing like your first love; right, Jack?"

Jack agreed.

Sunny was completely unnerved. She was shaking and thought she was going to throw up. She was so surprised by his presence she couldn't think straight. She didn't even recognize what she wrote on her pad. Her instinct was to run. She had to leave, now. She grabbed Sophia, the person she was closest with at work, and told her she felt very sick and needed to go home. Sunny begged her to take her table and let the manager know she was sick. She left.

Sunny ran all the way back to her apartment. She burst through the door and threw herself on her bed, burying her face in her pillow. When she started to breath at a more normal pace she was able to put together some cohesive thoughts. His face came to mind first. He looked the same but different. He looked happy. Maybe that was his girlfriend and he loved her. Why would he be in her restaurant? The pain of missing him surfaced again. Jack Johnson had left an imprint on her soul and the sight of him made her want him back, bad.

She sat on her bed, head in her hand and said out loud, "OH MY GOD I still love him." She threw herself back on the bed. "What is wrong with me? He has moved on and I still love him, what an idiot. Why do I still love him?" she kept saying things out loud while staring at the ceiling. She started to cry and couldn't stop, sad and angry with herself.

The waitress came back to the table with the drinks and Jack couldn't hide the disappointment.

Sophia said, "I'll be taking your lunch order, what can I get for you today?"

Jack was still trying to maintain his cool and place his order.

He finally asked, "What happened to our first waitress?"

"She wasn't feeling well so I am helping her out today," Sophia responded.

He excused himself and went to the bar area looking for her. The bartender asked him if he needed help.

"Yes, is Sunny here?"

The bartender looked puzzled, "I don't know sir, are you meeting someone?"

"No, Sunny the waitress. She was just at our table."

"I am sorry, sir; we don't have a waitress named Sunny. Is there anything else I can get for you?"

"The waitress that just took our drink order, Sunny." Jack motioned toward his table and his words sounded more rude than he intended.

"I think that is Sophia's table." The bartender waited on another customer.

Jack didn't know what to say. He couldn't figure out what was going on. Frustrated he went back to his table.

When Sophia came back he tried to sound casual. "What was our first waitress's name?"

Sophia cheerily said, "That was Rey. She's terrific and she trained me so I will take great care of you today. No worries." And she flashed a lovely smile that never reached her eyes.

Jack couldn't believe she was going by her middle name. She loved her name. Why would she do that? He didn't want to seem crazy to his coworkers by asking too many questions about Sunny. So he politely ate his meal and excused himself again and sought out Sophia.

She spied him first and came over to Jack. "What can I do for you?" she asked.

"I was wondering where Rey is and if I could speak with her?" It felt weird to call her Rey but he was trying to remain cool.

"She was feeling sick and went home." Jack stood there for a moment trying to figure out how he was going to get to Sunny.

"Do you think I could have her phone number?" Sophia was getting suspicious of this man.

"I am sorry but we cannot give our employee numbers." Jack decided to turn on his charm and weasel Sunny's whereabouts out of Sophia.

"I certainly understand, Sophia. But I knew Rey a long time ago and I would love to catch up with her. She and my sister were so close and she would hang around my house all the time. I really miss seeing her and I would love to tell my sister all about what she's up to since she left Seaville."

That last part caught Sophia's attention because she knew Rey was from Seaville so this guy must be for real. She took her pad out and started writing Sunny's number down.

"I am sure she won't mind." She was enamored with Jack's good looks.

He seized the moment. "You said she doesn't feel good?"

"Yes, she ran out of here fast. She must really have been sick. She has never left in the middle of a shift before."

"What if I brought her some soup and maybe flowers to make her feel better?" He laid it on thick and Sophia fell for it.

"That is very sweet. I bet she would love it." She added Sunny's address to the paper. "She doesn't live far."

Jack was overjoyed and mentally planned his next move.

Sunny was still reeling from seeing Jack. She was feeling stupid for running out of the restaurant like that. "Well, what's done is done." Then she laughed out loud at her mom's words were coming out of her mouth.

She was trying to sort out the epiphany she had about Jack. It had been buried deep the whole time and seeing him instantly brought it back. She truly believed that she had moved forward and perhaps she did, but she just didn't take into account her love for him was still so strong. She started gathering laundry. She might as well make the most of her extra time today. She placed her laundry basket beside the door and started a 'to do' list for the upcoming week. Sunny loved making lists and checking things off as she accomplished them.

She sat staring off thinking about the events of the day when she heard a knock at her door. When she touched the doorknob she felt a very familiar electrical impulse. She didn't have to open the door to know who it was because she could feel him. Jack.

Chapter 26

Sunny held the door for stability as she opened it. If she let go, she would crumple in a heap. Jack looked at his Sunshine like a starving man seeing a lavish buffet.

"Jack, how did you find me?"

"Sophia gave me your address after a little charm." Sunny stepped back to allow Jack in.

"I'm going to have to speak with her," she admonished.

"Please don't. I gave her a big story and sad face and she caved." Sunny let out a half giggle and Jack was close to dropping to his knees.

It was awkward and familiar at the same time. Sunny said, "Please come in and have a seat. Can I get you anything?" Her inherent good manners took over.

Inside Jack thought *yes, you, that's what I want.* He didn't want to blow this. He told himself to breath. "No thank you. How are you, Sunshine?"

Just the way he said her name made her want to throw herself at him and say take me I am all yours.

"I have been okay. Things are looking up for me. How are things with you, Jack?"

"I have a great job that I truly enjoy. It's a large firm here in the city here and I commute from Long Island." He gave her all the details of his job.

"Do you still live home?"

"Actually yes, I have been so focused on work that I never got around to finding my own apartment. And to be honest my family doesn't mind. My father told me to save my money for my dream home."

Sunny couldn't help but think about the woman she saw at the restaurant. "Was that your girlfriend?"

Jack was perplexed. "Who?"

"The girl you were next to at the table."

Jack smiled. "No, she's a coworker."

Sunny did a little happy dance inside. "So why did you charm my address out of Sophia. What do you want, Jack Johnson?"

Jack thought about all the things he could say and explanations he could render, and it came down to one thing.

"YOU."

"Excuse me?"

Jack looked at her with smoldering eyes. "You heard me. I want you, always have, always will."

Sunny thought she would explode. Her body took over and she stood up and walked over to him. "Me?"

He stood up too, took her in his arms, and kissed her. She reached up and put her arms around his neck. He had his arms around her waist, and they kissed as though it was the last kiss on Earth. When they came up for air, Sunny was crying.

Jack stepped back concerned that he had done something wrong. "Are you okay? What's wrong?"

"I have missed you so much that it h…"

She couldn't finish her sentence because his lips were back over hers. They devoured each other and all of the longing, hurt and love poured out into each other. Jack scooped her up and she wrapped her legs around his waist. She pointed toward the bedroom. He placed her down on the bed and looked at her as if she were his universe. Sunny's legs trembled. She was panting and they weren't even touching. Sunny couldn't wait. She sat up and started to undo the buttons on Jack's shirt. As she did, she kneeled on the bed and he stood beside it. His shirt hung open and she curled her hand around his neck. She made a trail of kisses up his throat and to his lips. The feel of his skin under her fingers was more electric than she remembered. Little pulses of excitement danced across their skin. Jack closed his eyes and absorbed the pleasure. He grabbed the hem of Sunny's shirt and removed it. As he kissed her shoulder, he undid her bra. She let it slip off. They were skin to skin now. Jack guided her back down, removed her pants and his own.

He slid next to Sunny running his hand across her hip, down her leg and up her inner thigh. She moaned and pulled him on top of her.

"Jack, I want you now, it's been long enough."

She wrapped her legs around him and he eased into her slowly. He let out a primal sound as he quickened his motion. She raised her hips to meet him as their bodies fused together. Jack mumbled her name against her throat until they were both shuddering and barely able to catch their breath. It took several minutes for them to float back down to reality. They were lying in each other's arms in disbelief.

Jack spoke first. "I can't believe this is real. It feels so good to hold you again. I feel like I have come home."

Sunny felt like this too, but there were questions she had to ask. She started to shift and he tightened his grip to keep her near. She maneuvered herself so she could look at him.

"I feel the same way but…" Jack started to stiffen, worried what was coming next… "I have questions and I can't move forward without answers."

Jack had some questions of his own. "Let's talk then." Sunny got up to get dressed and Jack pulled her back. "Can't we talk here?"

"No I cannot. I am distracted by your naked body, so get up." This pleased him to no end, and he happily complied.

As they sat in her apartment, he examined the room. The only thing he had seen before was Sunny, but now he wanted to see what she called home. It was small. The kitchen had painted cabinets and a Formica counter. There was a television on an end table; the couch he was sitting on and a small round table with two chairs. Family photos adorned the walls, including a beautiful picture of her and Kate with a date from last summer on it. There was a spattering of beachy décor as well. Something was missing.

"Where is your stereo?" Sunny didn't look at Jack.

"I don't have one."

"What? Why not?"

"Music made me more sad than happy for a while so I just didn't get one." Jack's heart constricted, she loved music so much and then it caused her pain, because of him.

"I know what you're thinking, Jack, but it was because of me, not you."

He smiled at her. "So now you can read my mind?"

"Kind of, it's what I would think. You see I didn't get the same enjoyment and for a while I just played our songs and that made me sadder. I would listen and cry my heart out for us, for the baby. I fell into a very dark place and I got to a point where I just didn't want to feel anything anymore."

Jack remembered what Joann told him but he wanted to know more from Sunny.

"I'm sorry that I left the way I did. I actually thought you would be at the airport the day I left."

"I thought you would say goodbye to me too, Jack. Why did you leave like that? This is the question that has haunted me. I felt like the sight of me disgusted you and you couldn't bear to look at me. I need to know now and I am ready to hear the truth, whatever it is."

Jack looked at her with disbelief. "The sight of you never disgusted me. In fact the opposite was true. I was so hurt and angry that you cut me out of such an important decision that I needed to not be near you so I could think straight. In your presence I am captured in your spell, I don't think clearly and I want to hold you and protect you at any cost, even my own feelings."

"Oh, Jack." Her voice cracked as she spoke. "I am so sorry for everything."

"I was and am consumed by my love for you. I think that's why I was so deeply crushed by you not trusting in me and making such an important decision without me."

"The last thing in the world I ever wanted to do was hurt you and I thought I was doing the opposite. You were my everything and I wanted you to have your dream. I knew how good you were and that you would feel obligated to marry me."

"I felt like I didn't matter to you and I just ran," Jack's voice wavered.

"I couldn't become an obligation and I was not ready to be a mom."

All the fear and despair she once felt rose again. She knew she had to talk it out to get through it but she never thought she would have this opportunity with Jack.

"I can never take back what I did, but do you think you can ever forgive me? It's unfair of me to ask and I understand if you can't, but I need to ask anyway."

Jack remained quiet for a couple of minutes, and Sunny was afraid of what his answer was going to be.

"There was a time when I would have said no, but time has made see things differently. I didn't fully understand how deep my love was for you until I was so far away, but I know this love is real. I have already forgiven you and I want to move forward *with you*."

Sunny got up from her chair and climbed into his lap. "Thank you, thank you."

The rest was unintelligible through her tears. It was the one missing piece she needed for her to completely forgive herself. Jack held her as she cried. He stroked her back and soothed her with kisses in her hair while whispering, "It will be okay now, let it out, Sunny." He wept with her. They held each other and cried for the hurt, the broken hearts and the baby.

They stayed like this until Jack's arms were numb and Sunny had no tears left. It was dark in the apartment now. Sunny got up and went to the bathroom.

She saw herself in the mirror and let out an "OH CRAP!"

Jack called out, "Everything all right?"

"My face is hideous. It's swollen and red from crying and I am not coming out until it goes down."

Jack came to the bathroom door laughing. "Let me see and be the judge of that."

When she opened the door he jumped back in mock horror, and she closed the door again. He came in slowly.

"Hey, you are beautiful inside and out. Come here." He pulled her to him and placed feather-light kisses around her swollen eyes.

"I can't believe I am in your arms again, Jack. This doesn't feel real."

Jack waited so long for this, being here with Sunny. Their reunion was more than he had ever hoped for. Jack could feel her body stiffen.

"What is it? Tell me."

He was more assertive than Sunny remembered, but he still knew what she was thinking.

"I need time, Jack. I think you should go. I have to process today."

"I just found my way back to you and don't want to go."

"Please, Jack, I am overwhelmed, emotional and I can't think straight. I need to figure out what I want."

Jack felt defeated, but he respected Sunny's wishes and he stood up. "I will go if you want me to."

"Thank you, Jack, seeing you today brought all my feelings back to the surface. I had them buried deep inside. I never thought I would get the chance to see you, let alone talk with you *and* have you forgiven me."

They went back into the living room and sat down. Jack took Sunny's hands.

"Whatever we need to talk about, let's do it now. I am not going anywhere in the foreseeable future, so you have my undivided attention."

Sunny inhaled, "I would like to start over with you but I am afraid. When I saw you today, I went into panic mode and my first instinct was to run as far away as possible. When I got back here, I realized how much I still love you. What if I do something incredibly stupid again and you run? I don't know if I can come back from that again."

"Sunny, I made a mistake. I regret leaving you like that. I called you from Italy and came right to your house when I got home only to find out the damage was done and you had moved on."

"I didn't know about the call, Jack. When?"

"After I settled in I couldn't get you out of my mind. As much as I needed space even being in a different country didn't stop the thoughts of you, so I called to try and talk with you. Your dad answered and he was pretty abrupt."

"My dad was beside himself then, and he felt so helpless he probably blamed you."

"I realize now why, but I didn't know any of that so I just assumed you no longer wanted any part of me in your life and so I didn't try to contact you again until I came home."

"I am so sorry, Jack."

"No more sorrys from you. It's not necessary. We are past that." His thumb gently rubbed her hand as he held it. "I also need to know something from you. I want you to promise me you will come to me when something is wrong and not shut me out. I think that together we can face anything."

"Please give me some time, please go now. I don't know if I'm ready to make promises. Just go, Jack."

Jack didn't say a word, he walked out the door and Sunny let him. Sunny sat on her couch thinking that in a couple of hours her life just changed. The man she loves still loves her and she just told him to leave.

"What is wrong with me?" She jumped up and headed for the door. She opened it to find Jack standing right there in the hall.

"Last time, I left and didn't look back and I have regretted that choice ever since. Today I decided I'm staying put. If I have to sit outside your door until you feel ready, I will. I am here."

"Jack, I love you so much, I'm sorry I asked you to leave because that is the last thing I want. Don't ever leave me again."

He put his arms around her and whispered, "I don't plan to. We will take it slow; I know you are afraid. We'll figure it out."

They stayed up all night talking and catching up on all the things they missed about each other the past few years. Jack asked Sunny what she would like to do after college. Sunny was uncomfortable for a moment before she answered.

"I want to be a counselor, specifically for teens."

Jack thought this was admirable. "Because of what you went through?"

"Yes. I had so many people who love me and I shut them all out. I'd never felt so alone and I didn't feel like I could talk to anyone especially my loved ones. It doesn't make sense. I didn't even tell Kate my deepest, darkest fears."

Jack kept his eyes locked on Sunny and he could see the pain as she spoke. He pulled her close and kissed her forehead. "I love you so much."

"I want to be there for teenagers who think no one else is." Sunny shrugged. "In a way my grandfather tried to warn me that I need to rely on the people who love me but I didn't listen."

Jack looked at Sunny strangely. He was pretty sure her grandfather had died. "Explain that please."

Sunny smiled and told him all about the call and her visit to Psychic Mike's house. Then it dawned on her.

"Do you want to hear something?"

Before Jack could answer she was on her feet running into her bedroom. Sunny rummaged through the drawer and Jack heard her exclaim, "Yes!" She came out with a cassette recorder and cassette.

"Promise me, you will keep an open mind, Jack."

Jack was intrigued. "Of course, I will."

Sunny played the tape of her session with Psychic Mike. She studied Jack's face as he listened. His expression changed and his eyes filled up. When the recording ended he looked into her eyes.

"It is strange but I believe him. I wonder what our son would have been like."

"I think about him all the time. I wonder what he would look like now."

"I hadn't really thought about the baby as a person until just now. But now I feel like our son is meant to be ours no matter what."

Sunny was relieved. "I feel the same way, like it is written in the stars. It lifted the guilt I had felt. I wondered if I would ever get the chance to meet him, and after tonight, I have hope again."

The sun was coming up by the time they were thoroughly talked out. Sunny got up to get a drink of water to soothe her dry throat. Jack approached and encircled her waist with arms as she stood at the sink. He started kissing her shoulder and neck. She leaned into him tilting her head to allow better access, this felt so good, so right. She let out a moan, she wanted her arms around him too but this felt too good to move. She turned to face him and he lifted her up onto the counter in one graceful move.

"I am finally home," he said, and he kissed her.

Sunny wrapped her legs around him. "This is where we belong, together. I love you."

He carried her to the bedroom and placed her down on the bed. Jack slowly removed her shirt savoring every movement, every touch. He was delighted to find she had not put a bra back on. He removed his shirt next and joined her. They held on to one another relishing the skin-to-skin contact, and without a word they removed each other's pants. Jack traced his finger down the length of Sunny's body. She shuddered with desire. Sunny kissed every square inch of his chest. This time, they languished over each other and made love until they were exhausted. They explored each other's bodies on their journey home.

Jack and Sunny were lying next to each other completely naked inside and out. They slept an undisturbed sleep in a tangle of limbs and love.

The next morning Jack opened his eyes and couldn't believe he was looking at Sunny. She looked gorgeous as she slept. He was torn between wanting to take her again and watching her sleep. Before he could decide she opened her eyes.

"Good morning, my love," Sunny whispered.

"I could get very accustomed to waking up like this. It is the best way to start a day." Jack's eyes twinkled and Sunny felt that clench deep inside. Decision made.

Chapter 27

During one of Sunny's regular phone calls home, Gary answered the phone and she told him about the reunion with Jack.

Through gritted teeth he said, "Sunshine, are you sure this is the right move?"

"Dad, we talked about everything. It's okay. Plus, I realized that I still love him with all my heart." Sunny could hear her father take a deep breath.

"I trust you. Why don't you both come for dinner next weekend?"

"Thanks, Daddy. I know that this is not easy for you and I really appreciate it. Jack and I agreed to take it slow." Sunny was hoping Jack was okay with the plans too.

He was, and things went as well as they could. At first, things were tense but they fell into a familiar ease of conversation. They caught up on the past few years and they could see the happiness in their daughter. She was happier than she had been in a very long time. After Sunny and Jack left, Joann and Gary sat in the living room.

"I believe she will be okay now. She has become this kind, levelheaded woman."

Gary smiled at his wife. "I am so proud of how far she has come."

"She has come into her own." Joann rested her head on her husband's shoulder.

The next weekend the couple went to Jack's house for dinner. His parents were so happy to see Sunny again. They knew how much their son had missed her when they had broken up. Charlotte and Edwin didn't know why they had broken up but they were glad to see them together again. Hannah wasn't as pleased.

"Hannah isn't feeling well, so she won't be joining us for dinner," Charlotte said.

"What is wrong with her, Mom?" Jack said with disbelief.

"I am not sure. Just leave her be, she will be okay." Jack started to stand up and Sunny placed her hand on his arm.

"Let me go check on her." She headed to Hannah's room before anyone could protest. Sunny knocked on the door.

"Hannah, may I come in?"

"Yea, I guess."

"Thanks, are you okay?"

"I don't feel like eating tonight, so you can go back and enjoy your reunion dinner." Hannah didn't look up from the magazine she was reading.

"Well before I do that I wanted to talk to you," Sunny spoke softly.

"So talk."

"When your brother and I broke up, I was distraught. I couldn't even take care of myself, let alone be a friend to anyone else. I missed my friends. But I was so sad I couldn't even talk with anyone, including you."

Hannah started to look at Sunny as she stood in front of the bed where she sat. Hannah was still quiet. Sunny decided to continue.

"I really missed you, Hannah, and I am very sorry that I hurt you, I hope one day you can forgive me. I am sorry."

Sunny silently left the room closing the door behind her. About halfway through dinner Hannah appeared and joined them at the table. Edwin smiled at his daughter.

"Glad to see you feel better, sweetheart."

Hannah returned the smile and filled her plate.

Chapter 28

In the ensuing weeks and months Sunny and Jack were inseparable. They were making up for lost time, taking it slow was forgotten. After work Jack would come by the restaurant, eat dinner at the bar and walk Sunny home. Before Jack started coming to the restaurant Sunny told him all about Paul. Sunny had talked to Paul when he returned from Fire Island.

"You look really happy, Rey. At one time I hoped it would be me, but I realized we didn't have that connection."

"You have been a great friend to me and I value that, Paul. I hope we can stay friends."

Paul gave her a hug. "I wouldn't have it any other way. When do I get to meet Mr. Wonderful?"

"He will be here when he gets off work."

The first time he met Paul was somewhat awkward. Jack actually liked him and he appreciated that he took care of Sunny too.

Some nights after Jack walked Sunny home he would take a late train home. Some nights he stayed with her in the city. Sunny hated when he left, so she asked him to move in.

"Are you sure you are ready for this, Sunshine Rey?"

He liked to add the Rey in every once in a while now. He also never called her *Sunny* at the restaurant. He liked *Rey*, the waitress; she made him smile.

"Yes, I want you here all the time. Every time I open my eyes I want to see your pretty face, Jack Johnson."

He batted his eyes. "Pretty huh?"

"Yes, you are very pretty to me!" As Sunny said it she bopped him with a throw pillow.

"Throwing things? Now, Miss Marino, I won't have that." He knocked her down on the couch. "We don't throw things at my pretty face. What if I got a black eye? This beauty would be damaged." He framed his face with his hands.

"Maybe a mark on that pretty face would tone down that conceit." She could barely get the words out; she was laughing so hard. "So, pretty boy, what's it gonna be? You moving in or what?"

Sunny was standing with her hands on her hips trying to look tough.

"I need to know what the *or what* will be first," Jack said matching her tough stance.

"The *or what* is none of this," she said as she made a sweeping motion down her body. "All of this will be off limits until you say *yes*!"

Jack couldn't resist teasing her. "Let me think about it, it's a very big decision."

Sunny started singing, "I gotta know right now, will you love me, will you love me forever?" She could not finish she was laughing so hard and Jack came to her and swept her up in his arms.

"You make quite a convincing argument, and since I really like all of this." He ran his hands down her body. "I guess I should move in."

Sunny let out a scream of delight, jumped up and wrapped her legs and arms around him. Oh how she loved this man.

Moving day was here! They purchased a new dresser together and Jack brought in boxes and bags. There was one box he wouldn't let Sunny touch. Jack was trying to conceal the words on the box which made her more curious. He made her take a seat on the couch.

"Sit down and close your eyes. No peeking or I won't show you."

Sunny was giggling. "Okay, Mr. Bossy Pants, they're closed. Hurry up!"

She heard him moving about, the box opening and what sounded like Styrofoam. It was making her antsy.

"Ready to open your eyes?"

"Yes, I can't wait anymore. Can I open them now? Please, please!" Sunny was laughing.

"Open your eyes, Sunshine Rey. SURPRISE!" Jack was standing next to a brand new, state of the art stereo system. It had a dual cassette player and a CD player. Sunny couldn't believe her eyes.

She jumped up shouting, "It is so beautiful! I can't wait to listen to something. Jack this is the best!"

Jack pressed play and *You're My Best Friend* started playing. Jack grabbed Sunny and started dancing around the apartment with her. Music once again filled their home and hearts.

Sunny and Jack loved living together and getting to know each other's daily habits. Jack thought it was adorable that Sunny would slip out of bed first thing in the morning to brush her teeth and snuggle back in. Sunny loved when Jack fell asleep spooning her. They shared in all the daily tasks such as laundry, cleaning and trips to the grocery store. Sunny and Jack took turns cooking and doing the dishes. They would prepare meals together, but sometimes dinner would be put on a back burner because making love came before making dinner. One evening *Walking on Sunshine* played on the radio and Sunny turned the volume up. She started dancing and singing all around, and Jack couldn't help but join in. They were captured in each other's spell.

Jack looked at Sunny and said, "You might as well face it. We're addicted to love."

The holidays were fast approaching and Sunny and Jack relished shopping for their own Christmas tree and all the decorations. Even though they were going to spend the actual days with their families, they loved creating their own traditions.

Christmas Eve, at The Marino house, Jack saw Kate for the first time since he and Sunny reunited. Kate cornered Jack alone.

"Listen, Jack, I know Sunny is happy and I am happy for her. I am still pissed off that you left her like you did. Don't let it happen again."

Jack reached for Kate, embraced her and placed a kiss on her forehead. "I have no intention of going anywhere. I am glad you are her friend."

Kate couldn't suppress her smile. She hugged him back. "Okay, I am glad we had this talk."

Sunny joined them putting her arm around Jack's waist. "Am I interrupting something?"

Kate replied. "Nope, I just had to have a talk with Jack, you two have my approval now."

Jack and Sunny responded, "Thanks."

After Christmas, Kate and Nate came into the city to spend the night and do some sightseeing. The foursome went to see the Christmas Tree at Rockefeller Center. It was a tremendous Norway spruce with hundreds of lights. Just standing under it made you feel like an ant.

They walked all around Rockefeller Center gazing at the angels that lined the square and bought roasted chestnuts from a street vendor. They sat together, eating the nuts and staring at the majestic tree. Jack, Sunny, Kate and Nate waited on the long line to rent skates. They finally got their skates and skated under the tree. It was a magical night. It reminded Sunny of their first date at the roller rink, and of course Jack was just as graceful on ice skates. They held hands as they skated. Sunny looked at the man she loved and the best friend she loved and thought how lucky she was to have this kind of love in her life.

"Jack, I love you."

He turned so he was skating backward and smiled at her.

"What's not to love baby!" He winked and skated off laughing.

When Jack was back at Sunny's side, he took her hand, "I love you heart and soul."

Sunny replied, "Of course you do. I expect nothing less."

They were so immersed in their joy they didn't notice Nate skate into the middle and get down on one knee. He produced a small box from his coat. All the skaters seemed to notice at once. Kate came to rest right in front of him.

"Kate Ackers, please do me the honor of being my one and only. Grow old with me, be the mother to my children and be the wife of my dreams. Please!"

Everyone on the ice was waiting for her to answer him. Kate beamed.

"Yes! Yes to all of that!"

She extended her hand and Nate placed the diamond ring on her finger. Kate and Nate stood in an embrace, kissing to applause.

"Jack, I am so happy that Nate let us share this, I am so excited for Kate I need to break that up so I can hug and kiss her too!"

"Skate slowly and give them a few minutes to enjoy their moment," Jack said smiling and following right behind her.

Sunny reluctantly complied and slowly made her way to Kate and Nate. When she reached the couple she squealed and hugged the both of them.

"Let me see that ring!" The girls oohhed and aahhed over the ring and Kate yelled out, "I'm getting married!"

Jack shook Nate's hand and he hugged Kate wishing her a long and happy marriage. They left the ice, purchased some champagne and went back to Sunny and Jack's place.

They were toasting to the couple when Kate said, "You have to be my maid of honor, Sunny!"

"I assumed I would be. Who else would you even consider?" and they burst into laughter. "Just pick out a dress that I look great in." Sunny got up and twirled as she said it. The girls started talking about all of the particulars of the wedding.

Nate and Jack went into the living room as the girls were talking about dresses, hair, colors etc.

Jack offered Nate a beer, "Had enough of the bubbly?"

"Yea, I'd love a beer," Nate replied.

"I guess they are a package deal." He couldn't take his eyes off Kate.

Jack handed him a bottle of beer and smiled as he looked at the two women. "You got that right." He clinked his bottle against Nate's. "I wouldn't want it any other way."

Kate and Sunny talked for hours, Jack couldn't keep his eyes open any longer and Nate conked out on the couch.

Kate looked at her friend. "You seem so content and happy. It's like you have a visible aura of love."

"Oh, Kate, thanks." Sunny sighed. "I love him more than I can even say."

"The joy you and Jack have feels infectious. You have come a long way, Sun."

"You stood by me, you helped me come back from wherever I was, if I didn't tell you, I love you! You are a wonderful friend, Kate."

"You are my sister, I will always be by your side, no matter what."

"If you didn't stick by me I couldn't wake up with Jack every morning now. This is more than I could have ever hoped for. I thank my lucky stars I have both of you."

They hugged each other and Kate looked at her friend. "Do you ever miss seeing the stars? I know you can see them in the city but it's nothing like home."

"Recently I have been missing it. I would love a star-filled night on the beach."

"I miss having you close, and I can't remember the last time we gazed together."

"Me either, I will have to come back to the island one night soon to get my fill. Plus I miss my parents too. The city is close but sometimes I feel out of touch. When I first moved here that was exactly what I needed, but now I'm not sure. We both work here so it's convenient at least."

Kate wished Sunny still lived up the block too.

"Maybe you will move back one day, Sunny."

"Who knows? This has been like our old sleepovers. Maybe one day…"

Chapter 29

Spring had arrived and Jack was planning to go to his parents' house a couple of weekends in a row to help his dad with work around the house. Sunny worked on the weekends, so she didn't mind. It made her proud of what a good son he was. That's probably what made him such a great boyfriend too. She should thank his parents for raising him. Hannah was off to college so they were lonely. It was good for Jack to get to spend time with his mom and dad. What Sunny didn't know was Jack's dad was actually helping Jack with a plan.

Sunny's birthday was approaching and she suspected Jack was hiding something. He wasn't the only one who could see into a mind. She had no idea of what he was up to though. Her birthday came and went without any surprises. She had a wonderful birthday all the same: her parents came in to the city and they all went out to dinner. Jack gave her a beautiful pair of earrings too. She still couldn't figure out what he was hiding though. It was driving her crazy but Mr. Ocean Eyes didn't give her a clue.

The Sunday after her birthday Jack asked her to take a ride to the east end of Long Island with him. He told her he had a potential client that wanted a house designed there and he wanted to take a look at the property. They took the Long Island Rail Road and Jack's dad met them at the train station with the Camaro. His dad kept that car in tip top condition; he never considered getting rid of it and Jack didn't want him to. He loved that car and truth be told so did Sunny. They dropped his dad home and were on their way. Jack headed to the Long Island Expressway and Sunny looked at him oddly.

"Aren't we going toward the Hamptons?"

Jack smiled at her and she spotted a twinkle in his eye. "Nope, we are going North Fork today."

"I just assumed big client meant the Hamptons."

"Sorry to disappoint my darling, but we are heading out to Baiting Hollow." Jack patted her hand.

Sunny look perplexed. "Where the heck is Baiting Hollow? I haven't heard of it and I lived on Long Island most of my life."

When Jack explained where it was, Sunny remembered a time when she visited a North Shore beach.

"It's on the North Shore? Ew, I hate the Sound beaches. They are full of rocks with almost no sand. You can't walk barefoot and there are no waves. What kind of beach is that?"

She thought that Jack started to look nervous but she dismissed it. She went on.

"Didn't I read somewhere that they are making wine out here somewhere? I think there is some kind of vineyard around here. We should try and find it when we are done, I'd like to check it out."

Jack just nodded in agreement and kept his attention on his driving.

It felt like they were driving for hours, they drove to the end of the Long Island Expressway and continued further east. Jack made several turns and Sunny started to wonder why he didn't even refer to a map. He turned down this quiet street and drove to the end. Jack pulled onto a lot at the end of the block. It was partially wooded. He got out of the car and came around to Sunny's door and offered her his hand. She took it and got out with him. He led her through some brush and a clearing that came into view.

As Sunny walked farther onto the property, the most magnificent view was visible. They stood on a bluff overlooking Long Island Sound. There were sweeping views of the water from east to west.

She looked at Jack. "WOW. These views are amazing."

He was smirking and said, "Even for the lousy rock beach?"

She giggled. "In spite of the lousy rock beach."

They walked over to the edge of the bluff and there was a staircase that led to a beach that wasn't so rocky. Sunny looked out over the water.

"Jack, this is unbelievable. Whoever gets to live here and look at this all the time is so lucky. What are you thinking about for the house?"

She turned to look at him and he was on his knee with a jewelry box in his hand. The sun cast a glow on his face that took her breath away.

"How would you like to be the one who lives here happily ever after with me?"

Sunny couldn't believe what she just heard. "What? Here? What do you mean? Jack?"

"Sunshine Rey Marino, I want you to marry me and live here forever. This is ours. Yours and mine. I will build our dream house here, so don't leave me hanging. Yes or no? Will you marry me?"

Sunny kneeled down in front of him, "Of course I will marry you, I'm a given." She threw her arms around him and kissed him.

"Don't you want the ring?" Jack asked as he opened the box.

"Jack Johnson, I would marry you with or without a ring, but yes let me see that thing!" He placed it on her finger and she was awestruck. It was a marquis shaped diamond with three baguettes on each side. It was set in platinum and it was huge.

"Jack, this is beautiful and way too much and I am never taking it off!"

Jack hugged her tight and whispered. "You deserve a ring as beautiful as you. Want to see our house?"

Jack took her by the hand and walked her over to an area where she could see outlines in the grass. As she got closer she realized old logs and large branches outlined the footprint of a house. She looked at Jack.

"When did you buy this land, Jack? And when did you make the log house?"

"The weekends I was coming out to help my dad, we were actually cleaning up this lot and I had the idea to outline the house. My dad gave this lot to me as a college graduation gift. My grandfather left it to him and he had intended on living here one day, but it never happened. He knew I wanted to build my own dream house one day and he decided to give it to me. I want to build the home we raise our children in right here. What do you think, will you leave the city?"

"Jack, I would live at the end of the world as long as it was with you."

Jack kissed her. "Wait here."

Jack ran to the car and came back with a bag from the trunk that had all the provisions for a perfect picnic. They ate and made love in the orange glow of the sunset. It was pure magic. They gazed up as the stars started to emerge for the night and Sunny and Jack thanked their lucky stars they had each other.

They drove home and on the drive Jack played *Heaven* for her.

"This song sums it up. You are all that I need," he said and he brought her hand up to his lips.

When they arrived at Jack's house, Sunny noticed her parents' car and looked at Jack. Everyone was there to congratulate them; her parents, Kate, Nate and Hannah too.

"You did all of this? This is the second-best day of my life. I love you!"

Jack gave her a look. "The second-best day? Really? What exactly was the first?"

"Wipe that look off your face because the best day of my life was the night I was sitting alone by the pool looking at the stars and I met you."

Sunny wrapped her arm around his waist and snuggled against him. The champagne was poured and passed out. Everyone toasted the couple. Jack and Sunny mingled and chatted with everyone.

Sunny went over to Hannah to thank her for coming home and hugged her as she whispered in her ear, "I am so glad you will be my sister-in-law. I couldn't ask for anyone better."

Hannah was happy for them, and when she returned the embrace she meant it, her hurt forgotten. "Me too, Sunny."

Kate got her friend alone for a minute and asked her a question.

"Have you thought about a date yet?"

Sunny pushed her friend in a playful way. "No, I have been engaged a couple of hours. We have not even discussed it."

Kate said half joking. "There's room next to me on New Year's Eve."

"Kate, I love the wedding plans you have made so far, but they are yours. You shouldn't share your day with me. Besides I don't know if I can wait until New Year's. I think a summer beach wedding will suit us just fine."

Gary sat down next to Jack.

"I appreciate your asking for my blessing to marry Sunny and I want you to know that the past is just that, the past. You put together this whole day to make it special for my daughter. She is truly happy. Thank you Jack." And he extended his hand to Jack who took it and shook it.

Jack tried to swallow the lump in his throat. "I appreciate it Mr. Marino and I plan on putting forth my best effort for Sunny every day of my life."

Chapter 30

Sunny and Jack became Mr. and Mrs. Johnson on a beautiful Saturday in early September, 1986. They promised their lifelong love at the little beach by the bay. Sunny stood before Jack in an ankle length, lace dress. It had a sweetheart neck line and cap sleeves. She looked like an old-fashioned Hollywood movie star. It was not white; it was the palest gold and it made her hair glisten as it hung in spiral curls around her shoulders and down her back. The only thing on her feet was the dangle of a gold ankle bracelet. Jack wore a black suit, a crisp white shirt and a tie that matched Sunny's dress exactly. The bottom of his pants exposed his bare feet.

They held hands facing each other, Jack went first.

"Sunshine Rey Marino, the night I met you under the stars I knew I was yours. You captured my heart before I knew what was happening. I stand here before you and everyone we love, promising to love you heart and soul for the rest of our lives and to always be worthy of you. I promise to always listen and communicate with you. We will take on life side by side because together is always better. I will love you as long as the stars shine."

Sunny let the tears roll down her face. His words wrapped around her like a blanket of love. She smiled and kissed his cheek.

"My turn. Jack Johnson, I have never felt happier than this very moment. I thank my lucky stars that we met. You are my best friend, you are my partner, you are the love of my life. You are the man I will share my life with. I promise to be open and honest with you always and to take our life's journey by your side. I know I can live without you and I also know that living with you is so much better, it is pure joy. I love you heart and soul, Mr. Johnson."

When they were pronounced husband and wife everyone clapped and no one had to tell Jack to kiss his bride, he had it under control.

They all went back to the Marino home and celebrated. Joann and Gary transformed the backyard into a magical garden. They had plenty of help. Hannah and Kate were there all week helping with every detail. Sunny wanted to help but her mother insisted it be a surprise. Gary set up music for the entire party. He asked Jack and Sunny for a selection of songs they would like, and set out on the task as if it was a soundtrack for a major motion picture.

Sunny and Jack had to wait until everyone was in the yard before they could enter. They were waiting for the okay, and Jack took Sunny's face in his hands.

"This is the happiest day of my life. I can't believe we are married and I will do everything in my power to never let this feeling go away. I love all of you with all of me." He kissed her; a kiss that made her senses go into overdrive.

She wrapped her arms around him and deepened the kiss, they were lost in each other.

"Would you two like to come up for air for a minute and join the party?" Hannah said with mock disgust.

"Sorry I just can't help it sometimes; your brother makes me forget my good manners. Now let's see our surprise!" Sunny gave Hannah a hug and kiss before her sister-in-law escorted them in to their reception.

The vision that met their eyes would stay in their memory forever. Candles flickered, lights twinkled, tables were topped with linen and flower petals. Tiny white lights hung all over, soft, flowing curtains made of tulle were tied back with white ribbons; and flowers were everywhere, even lilacs. Sunny had no idea where her mom found them in September, but she did. There was a dance floor. There was not a detail left out. It was perfect. It brought tears to Sunny's eyes. Jack was taken with how lovely everything looked and how much work went into what was before his eyes, he could barely swallow the lump in his throat. It was an enchanted garden just for them.

They had their first dance to *Heaven.* Jack whispered the words to the song into Sunny's ear, and she felt like she was floating. Everyone else joined them on the dance floor to share their moment. When the song ended they embraced, one by one. The night was more than they had ever hoped for. Jack led his mom to the dance floor and as they danced to *Have I Told You Lately,* he thanked her for being the wonderful mother that she was and told her how much he loved her. Charlotte Johnson had to officially let her son go, but she was happy for him. She knew that Sunny was the right one for him.

Gary looked around the yard for his little girl. He picked a very special song to dance with her. He took Sunny by the hand.

"It's time to dance with your old dad." He gave her a wink.

"I would be honored to dance with my very young and handsome father. Let's dance." Gary gave his daughter a spin as *Greatest Love of All* started.

"Sunshine, you are the greatest love of my life and I am so proud of the woman you have become…" The rest of the words became lodged in the lump in his throat. They finished the dance in silence.

When the song ended, Sunny held her dad's hands. "Thank you for always being on my side and being the best dad I could ever ask for. I love you, Daddy." She kissed his tear-stained cheek.

Brown Eyed Girl brought everyone to their feet and there was not a square inch of the dance floor that Gary built left. Jack pointed at Sunny across the dance floor.

"You're my brown eyed girl, forever!"

She mouthed, "Yes I am," and burst into laughter and kept dancing with Kate. The Rolling Stones medley kept everyone dancing until their legs hurt. A couple of slower songs came on and Joann invited Jack's father to dance. As they danced, Jack came over and asked to cut in. Edwin handed Joann's hand to him and gave his son a hug.

Jack smiled at Joann, "I thought I should have at least one dance with my new mother-in-law."

Joann winced. "Eww, I don't like how that sounds. I no longer sound cool." She shrugged. "I guess it will take some getting used to."

"I still think you're very cool," Jack said with his most charismatic smile.

"I'm glad for this moment, I wanted to talk to you." Joann hesitated when she saw Jack's face fall, then she went on, "Don't worry, Jack. It's good stuff. Remember our talk when you returned from Italy?" Jack nodded, not sure of where this was going. "I told you to move on and leave Sunny alone because I was in full protection mode. I told you to be worthy of her belief in you." Jack was quiet but still dancing and Joann kept speaking. "Thank you for respecting me that much. It says so much about your character and how good you are. You are worthy, Jack. You make my daughter so happy and that gives me such peace of mind. Mr. Jack Johnson, I am proud to be your mother-in-law." She hugged him hard. Jack didn't know what to say, so he just hugged her back. This was the best night of his life.

The last song of the night was *You're My Best Friend*. They all knew the words and sang along as they danced The stars were shining so bright that night over the party it was as though everything was aligned the way it should be and the stars twinkled in agreement.

Chapter 31

Sunny and Jack reveled in their marital bliss. Anyone who was in their presence could feel the joy. Jack spent every spare minute designing their home. He would pour over the plans asking Sunny's opinion on each detail. She could watch Jack for hours. He truly loved what he did and Sunny hoped one day she would feel like that about her job. Sunny was trying to figure out where to apply for her master's degree, and she was going over her options when Jack came home.

"Hello, Sunshine. How was your day?" He planted a big kiss on her lips with a loud smacking sound making her giggle.

"Hello yourself, handsome. I am trying to stay cool in this August heat and figure out where I should get my master's."

"What do you think about one of the great colleges out on the island?" Jack said.

"Oh yeah, I'll go to school out there and run back here to work. You're brilliant," she said with a tone of sarcasm.

"What if we lived close by?" Jack was holding her gaze waiting for the opportunity.

"Where, Jack, on the plot of land in a tent? I am not living in a tent until our house is built, I don't care how much I love you."

Jack started laughing. "I can see this is not going how I expected. My company is opening a satellite office out east to better service our East End clients, and they have asked me to run it."

Sunny jumped up and onto Jack wrapping her legs around him. "That is fantastic! I am so proud of you. Oh my God, we *will* have to move!"

Jack kissed her, "I know, that's what I was trying to tell you, but you were not playing along. Let's figure out where we want to live until our house is built."

They were looking at a map of Suffolk County when the phone rang.

"I got it," Sunny said. She picked up the phone, paused and then said, "We will be on the next train."

Jack looked up at her and got that bad feeling in the pit of his stomach.

"It's your dad. He had a heart attack." All the color drained from his face, so she went to him and held him tight. "I'll pack a bag and we will head to Penn." Sunny quickly called her parents to pick them up at the station.

The train ride seemed to take hours. Jack just stared out the window and Sunny didn't know what to do or say. She wasn't about to tell him it would be okay because Charlotte had sounded terrible and Sunny was afraid that maybe Edwin was gone. Sunny sat by his side and held his hand; it was all she could do.

Joann was at the station standing outside her car as the train pulled in. She hugged them both and drove them straight to the hospital. Joann sat in the waiting room as Sunny and Jack went to find his parents.

They saw Charlotte sitting alone in an empty ER cubicle. Jack called out to her, "Mom, where's Dad? How is he? What happened?" The worry on her face was evident.

"It is serious, Jack. He had a heart attack and they just took him for some tests. They are talking about blockages and surgery and balloons. I'm so glad you two are here," she held both of their hands.

"Have you talked to Hannah?" Jack asked.

"I wanted to wait to have some answers but I think we should call her now," Charlotte said.

"I will take care of it," Sunny sprang into action, glad there was something she could do to help. She went out to the waiting room to talk with her mom. They asked the receptionist where the pay phones were and headed to a small room where they could make calls. They were thankful for the privacy. Sunny called the college and spoke with several different people. She finally got someone who assured her she would track Hannah down and get her to call the number provided.

"I'll wait by the phone, Sunny. Go back in to let them know and see if there is any news."

"Okay, Mom, thank you so much." She hugged her mother and whispered, "Please don't let anything happen to you and Daddy." Joann kissed her knowing that was a promise she couldn't make.

Sunny made her way back to her husband and mother-in-law, and just as she got there the doctor was walking over to them. Sunny knew the news was bad when she saw the doctor's face.

"Mrs. Johnson, your husband suffered another heart attack during the test. It was massive and despite our best efforts, he did not make it. I am very sorry for your loss." The doctor placed a hand on Charlotte's arm in a gesture of support. Sunny thought it was condescending. She immediately positioned herself in between Jack and Charlotte, holding them both.

Jack was stunned, she could feel the thoughts firing off in his head. Charlotte started to buckle at the knees, but Sunny grabbed her before Jack even realized what was happening. The doctor showed them to a private room. Sunny held Charlotte up and Jack followed behind. She brought her mother-in-law to a chair. She turned to Jack and put her arms around him and he broke down. Sunny held him while he cried whispering how sorry she was.

Back in the little phone room, the phone rang. It was Hannah.

"Hello," Joann said.

"Hi, this is Hannah Johnson, who is this?"

"Hannah sweetie, it's Joann."

"What's wrong and where are you?" Joann could hear the panic in her voice.

"Hannah, your dad had a heart attack and we're at the hospital." Hannah had a thousand questions.

"Is he okay?" she barely squeaked the question out.

"We don't know anything yet. They are running tests."

"I need to come home. I can't be here worrying, I need to find a way home, Joann."

"I understand, Hannah. I'll have Gary come get you. Don't worry, sweetheart. We will get you home. Can you give me the phone number where I can call you back?"

With one phone call, Gary was on his way. Joann knew she could count on him always. She let Hannah know to get ready and that Gary would be there soon.

As she was going back to the waiting room, she saw Sunny who motioned to her. She took her mom by the hand and went back to the *crying room*. It seemed to be the place they took people to so they could tell them their whole world is now different. Joann sat with Charlotte as Sunny tried to console Jack. He hadn't said a word since the doctor spoke to them.

Charlotte looked up suddenly. "Oh no, Hannah."

"I spoke with her earlier, and Gary is on his way to pick her up." Charlotte looked relieved for a fleeting moment, but she then realized she would have to tell her daughter that her father died.

Jack and his family went through the motions of performing all the tasks required of them during this time. Sunny took charge and took care of everything, she was a rock. She made sure they ate, slept, dressed on time and she even tucked little packs of tissues in their pockets. Sunny handled arrangements, paperwork, phone calls and anything else that came up. Jack hardly spoke this whole time, but when Sunny held him at night, he let her. The day of the funeral, everyone went back to the Johnson home. Sunny had ordered food and Joann got all the rest of the necessities. Kate and Nate went back to the house after the service to get everything ready. Gary drove everyone to and from.

They had become one big family. Sunny and Jack's love connected them all, and it was evident to anyone who took notice. They stood at the cemetery saying their last goodbyes and Sunny thought about Edwin looking down at them holding his grandson's hand. It gave her comfort.

When the last of the guests left the house, Sunny and Kate cleaned the kitchen. Every last dish had been washed, garbage taken out, food packed away and the floor was swept. Sunny looked at Kate.

"Wow, I can't believe it's done."

Kate smiled at her friend and hugged her, "Sunny, take a break. You have been taking care of everyone, and you need a rest."

"I know, but I can't just yet. I am so worried about Jack. He has barely said four words since his father died and I'm scared."

Kate handed Sunny her car keys. "Take him out of here for a little while. I've got this and your dad will give me and Nate a ride home, I love you, Sun. Now go."

"Thank you. What would I do without you? I love you." She went into the living room and took Jack by his hand.

"Let's go for a ride." He silently followed his wife.

Sunny drove to their spot, parked the car and turned to look at her husband. He looked lost and she needed to find him.

"Jack, you have not said much since the hospital, I gave you your space but I don't want you slipping away. Please look at me." He turned to face her with full eyes, and her heart constricted. She wanted nothing more than to take away his hurt.

"No running, Jack. Remember? I am here and I want you to share your feelings with me. I know how easy it is to withdraw into yourself, but please don't. I love you too much to not do everything in my power to keep you here."

He turned to look out the window again. She could feel him start to run within himself. She was scrambling in her own head trying to figure a way to reach him. She climbed onto his lap, straddling him so she could look right into his eyes.

She cupped his face, "Jack Johnson, I know you are hurt, I will share your hurt, I will even take it all if I can. I need you, please talk to me. I love you so much and this is killing me, I feel useless."

The last statement got to him. She was so far from useless. If not for her nothing would have gotten done. She was everything to him, but it was just that he hurt so much he was afraid to open up. It might break him.

In a barely audible whisper he said, "You are not even close to useless, you are my rock."

Sunny's sharp intake of breath echoed in the confines of the car. She encircled his head with her arms. "Oh Jack, thank you."

They sat quietly for a while before Jack spoke.

"I am afraid to acknowledge my feelings right now. I might not be able to handle it."

"I will handle it with you. I am scared if you don't let it out you will slide into a dark place that is very hard to return from."

Jack realized this must be a lot like how she felt after the abortion. Loss is loss. He reflected on their wedding vows, together is better and leaning on each other is right. They had come too far.

"When we got the phone call and I heard your voice I knew something bad happened. I was pleading with God or whoever could hear my prayers, for my father to be okay."

Sunny held him as the words trickled out. "Me too, Jack. I loved your dad from the moment he invited me to come to parents' weekend."

Jack smiled at the memory. He kissed Sunny on her hand. "That was a great weekend. It was my dad's idea to invite you because he knew you were the one."

He talked and cried, Sunny listened and soothed him. Edwin smiled down on them and the boy holding his hand had the same smile, they felt the love.

Chapter 32

After Edwin's death, Charlotte was lost. Hannah took a leave from school to grieve and Charlotte numbly went about her days. Sunny suggested that instead of getting their own place, they should move in with Charlotte and Hannah. Jack was grateful. He felt he needed to take care of his mother and sister. He was so thankful for his wife. Sunny knew that this was what they needed to do right now and everything would work out the way it needed to. They would take things one day at a time.

Everyone at the restaurant took Rey out to say goodbye. She had made many friends in the five years she worked there and she would miss them. The day they left the apartment Sunny looked around at the place where she found herself and started a new life. It held so many memories. She had tears in her eyes as she closed the door, but she was ready for the next chapter in her life. She wasn't sure what her future held, but she was okay with that.

Jack and Sunny moved in with Charlotte and Hannah. Once they were settled in Jack made Sunny promise to continue her education and not to look for a job.

"Focus on finishing your master's. You've got a lot of internships and other things that need completing. You don't need to work too. Besides everything you have been doing for us is a job all by itself. You need to take care of you. You have taken care of all of us when we couldn't do it ourselves and you have done it all with love."

"I am happy to help. I feel like I make a difference. I don't think about it, I just do what needs to be done. It is how we take care of each other. And I think I would feel weird not working."

Jack took her into his arms and put his finger on her lips. "Shhh, let me do this for you. I know you don't think about it and that's one of the reasons I love you so much. I want you to put all your effort into school. Then when you finish, find whatever job makes you happy." He planted a loud smacking kiss on her lips.

Sunny giggled and Jack said, "Oh no, you're giggling. That does wicked things to me." He swept her up in a passionate kiss as they made their way to the bedroom.

Sunny immersed herself into her studies and in December, 1989 she received her master's degree. When she walked across the stage to accept her degree, all the people she loved were there to celebrate her. They were so proud of her. Jack stood there beaming with biggest bouquet of flowers Sunny had ever seen. "Please make way for my beautiful and extremely smart wife."

As Sunny was pursuing career opportunities, Jack successfully ran the East End office as well as overseeing every detail of their dream house. Jack and Sunny would make weekly visits during the construction. Some Sunday mornings they would bring their coffee and lawn chairs to sit in their yard overlooking the Long Island Sound and dream of their future.

"Sunny, I want you to stop coming here for a while." Jack looked serious as he said this. Sunny couldn't believe what she was hearing.

"Are you kidding me? Why?"

He looked at her. "Do you trust me?"

"No Jack, I wouldn't trust you as far as I could throw you." She stuck her tongue out at him.

He took her hand, "I want the finished house to be a surprise to you. We come here all the time to monitor the progress, but I want to see your reaction to the finished product."

"I will miss our Sunday mornings."

"Every detail I have designed has been with you, us and our family in mind, and I want the joy of seeing you experience it." How could she possibly argue with that? She agreed.

The day had come. The house was complete. Jack could not have been more pleased with the result, and he could not wait for Sunny to see it. He had planned this day out a hundred times in his mind, but now that it was here he was nervous. As he drove, Sunny's excitement mixed with his nerves. He pulled in the driveway and looked at Sunny. The smile on her face that made her eyes twinkle was all he needed to calm his nerves. He walked around to her side of the car, took her hand, and led her to the door of their home.

She placed her hand on the dark wood door admiring it. She let her fingers graze across the semi-circle of stained glass. It reminded her of the beach; perhaps it was the colors. The foyer was open to the second floor and sunlight poured through the skylight. The tile they had picked out was installed in a pattern that accented its' beauty. As they made their way into the living room Sunny was soaking up every detail. She was afraid to step on the wood floors.

"Go ahead, you won't scratch them." Jack nudged her forward.

"I don't even want to put furniture on them, they are magnificent." She slipped her shoes off anyway. She padded into the kitchen. "What should our first dinner be in our new home? I will be able to see into every room…" Sunny slowly turned toward the sunlight gleaming in from where a wall should have been.

Jack couldn't contain himself anymore. "Surprise!"

Off the dining area and adjacent to the living area was a glass room that was not on the plans. She looked at Jack and went to the room. It was an atrium room with tiled floors, fireplace and most importantly a glass ceiling.

"Jack, this room is amazing! It feels so…us. I can see us curled up in front of the fireplace…" Before she could finish her sentence, Jack finished it for her.

"…gazing at the stars."

"On the coldest winter night, we can snuggle right here and star gaze."

"Oh Jack, just when I think I can't love you more, I do. You are the most perfect husband in the world and our life is the best love story in the world."

That night they made love right there in the atrium, under the stars.

Nine months later, Jack was at Sunny's side coaching her through her contractions. He held her hand and whispered how beautiful she was.

He caressed her head. "You can do this, Sunshine." Minutes seemed like hours. Watching her go through this was tearing him apart, he wanted to just take the pain away.

He placed ice chips on her lips and kissed her face. "We are going to get to meet our baby soon, our baby."

He had his arms around her as she was pushing, all the time telling her how much he loved her.

When the doctor held the baby up and proclaimed, "It's a boy."

Sunny and Jack looked at each other smiling and said, "we know."

He was the little boy they knew would be theirs one day. He was the boy who patiently waited until all of the stars aligned so he could make his entrance.

Epilogue

That boy was me. I am Ray Edwin Johnson, the one and only son of Jack and Sunny Johnson. And yes, I am named Ray as in *ray of sunshine.* My mother couldn't help herself and my father liked the name Ray. Fortunately, they kept the sunshine part private. Only a select group of people know that truth.

Even though I am an only child, I have plenty of family. My cousins are like my own siblings in many ways. Aunt Kate and Uncle Nate had four sons, four years in a row. My mom always said Aunt Kate had the patience of ten saints. Michael is the oldest, and my closest friend and then there is Christopher, William and Nate Jr. I know he should have been first but I think they just ran out of names. We were always together growing up, holidays, barbecues, weekend fun and the annual back yard event my parents hosted. My parents went all out, they hired a cook, wait staff, a DJ and always some type of children's entertainment from inflatable rides to magicians.

Everyone we knew was invited to the event, and it usually ended with my mom and Aunt Kate singing karaoke until our ears were bleeding. My father and Uncle Nate encouraged them too! Sometimes they all sang together; it was usually some Rolling Stones song. As kids we loved the fun, and as teenagers we were embarrassed of our parents. As adults we loved to join them.

Most of our vacations were with Aunt Kate and Uncle Nate just like my grandparents had taken them to Fire Island together every summer. Looking back, I appreciate all of it. As a child I sometimes wished I could just have my own vacation with my own family, but now I wouldn't trade one memory for a solo family vacation. My cousins and I became as close as brothers and remain that way.

Aunt Hannah and Uncle Thomas have two daughters who are younger than me, Cassandra and Lily. They actually moved to the same block as us and my father designed their home too. My grandfather left Aunt Hannah property on the same street. Cassandra and Lily were always around and that was fine with me. I adored both of them and also kept a watchful eye on them when they became teenagers and started dating. I always had final approval.

I met my wife through one of their friends. We met in junior high school, and instantly I knew Ava was my soul mate. I consider myself lucky to have found love like I did and I think it's because I had excellent role models.

I grew up in a house full of love. That was my normal so I assumed that's how every kid grew up. My mother always told me that we were the luckiest family ever because it was written in the stars for us to be together. We would go outside at night or just sit in our family room and recite, "Starlight, star bright first star I see tonight, wish I may, wish I might, get this wish I wish tonight."

My mother would say, "You take my wish because all of my wishes were granted, I have you and Daddy." It was like some hokey television show, but it was real at my house. It wasn't until I was older that I started to notice that not all families were as happy and loving. When I was in third or fourth grade there was a girl in my class who had to leave our school because her father went to jail, her parents were divorcing and she was going to have to live with her grandmother. I was shocked by this.

One day I asked my mom, who was a school counselor, "What happens to kids with no mom and dad around to love them?"

She smiled one of her smiles that always soothed me, and said, "Sometimes they just have to grow up anyway and try and be the best they can be." She kissed the top of my head, hugged me, and let me know that I would never have to worry about that. I accepted this as the truth. I became more observant.

It wasn't uncommon to see my father bound through the house from work or another room and grab my mother and start dancing to some song he just heard. One particular day stands out in my memory; I was about twelve, my father came bursting through the door calling my mother's name. I was in the kitchen with my mom as he whisked her into his arms singing, *Only wanna be with you.*

"Excuse me, Ray. The song was playing in my car and I just got caught in the moment. Your mom has that effect on me." They laughed, danced and swept me up with them, that joy stuck with me, even though at twelve years old, I was grossed out by their public display.

Music was a big part of our lives. The day my mother got her first MP3 player you would have thought she had discovered the cure for cancer. She couldn't stop talking about all of the features and everything she could store on it. My father and I had to laugh at her because she was talking so fast with such excitement. She had a playlist for everything; she became obsessed!

My mother was always singing some song or another to me too. Her favorite song that she always sang to me was *Everything I Do I Do It For You,* sometimes with tears in her eyes. On my wedding day, it was the song I danced with her to. I also dedicated a special song to my parents. The moment I had heard it I knew it was the perfect song for them. As *Thinking Out Loud* played, they stared into each other's eyes while mouthing the words to one another. They looked like the newlyweds.

My wife looked at me and said, "I plan on being in love with you like that for my whole life."

I kissed my wife and agreed with tears in my eyes.

We all loved to *give* each other songs and it wasn't until I was sitting with my mom during her chemotherapy sessions I found out the origin of the tradition and its' significance. I thought it was just a family thing.

The day my mom was diagnosed with ovarian cancer we were walking to the car with the humid mist of the summer day stuck to our skin, and she looked at my dad and I and said, "I am going to beat this frigging cancer, I am not leaving either one of you yet."

"We will help you beat this frigging cancer because we aren't ready to let you go," I said.

From day one, she met it head on. My mother was determined. She confided in me that she wanted me to write the story of their love, not because she thought she was going to die but just in case she did. She wanted her future grandchildren to know her and the legacy of love that they come from. That is how she put it to me. How could I say no to her? She was my mom and I am a writer. I am a sports writer, but I knew I would figure it out.

I sat with her during chemo or home afterward and I always brought pen and paper to take notes. I also made digital recordings of some of the sessions because I truly was mesmerized by their story. I learned so much more about my parents, I relished every single moment I got to spend hearing their love story, it truly was wonderful. I loved both of them more with every session. I was honored to be able to know my parents in a different light.

I made it my mission to gather and research as much as I could about my parents. I interviewed my grandparents, aunts and uncles, went to visit Fire Island and the little beach where my parents were married. I was able to get to know everyone in my life better, deeper, especially my Grandfather Edwin who I am named after. I am sad I didn't get to know him while he was alive but I have always had the feeling I somehow knew him; I could never explain it.

If she wasn't telling me all about the *best love story ever*, she was listening to a playlist she made to keep her motivated and focused. She also made a playlist of for our lives. It was long, but it had every song that had any importance to us. My father was beside her every step of the way with the exception of a short period of time. My mom had a reaction to her treatment and was hospitalized for ten days. She was still weak when she returned home. He began to stay at work longer or find excuses to run an errand. I thought the stress was too much for him and he started becoming sullen and withdrawn. I didn't know what to do or how to handle it.

I came home one day and found him sitting with my mom crying. I stepped out but I heard her telling him to stop running. I wasn't sure what she was talking about but it was after that day he started to come back around. He was her rock. My father kept vigil by her side during the worst of times and celebrated each triumph. Together we beat the cancer. My mother grew stronger, the smile started to come back to both of their eyes, the music was back in our lives. The stars once again aligned to make things right.

My children had the opportunity to have the most awesome grandparents in their lives. They had special sleepovers, vacations and just plain fun with them.

Many years later my phone rang early one morning and as soon as I touched it I had a very bad feeling. My first instinct was that my mom had died, and I was relieved to hear her voice on the phone. My relief was short lived because she had called to tell me my father didn't wake up that morning. He had died quietly in his sleep.

I was devastated and I felt my heart shatter inside my chest. I was sobbing and couldn't stop. My wife put her arms around me and held me until I could catch my breath. You can never imagine your life without your parents until it happens and nothing seems right about the world ever again.

It was a beautiful autumn day when my father was buried. There were so many people at his funeral. He was such a loved and wonderful man. People shook our hands, whispered condolences and patted my back, nodded at my children and hugged my mom. I went through the motions of everything. It seemed surreal. My mother and I were the last ones at the grave where we would have to leave my father. There were so many flowers on the casket you could no longer see the wood. We walked side by side silently, neither of us really wanting to leave without him. As we approached the car where my family was waiting, she stopped and I looked at her.

She took both my hands and said, "Please promise me one day you will write the best love story ever about the luckiest family there ever was. Ray, you are a good man, a good father and loving husband. You are the best son I could have ever dreamed of having, and I am the luckiest person in the world to have been your mother, your children's grandmother and Jack Johnson's wife."

I made that promise to my mother. The hours I spent interviewing my mom and my dad are in my heart forever. I loved hearing the story of how our family came to be. I always knew we were a happy family but it wasn't until I heard the stories that I really understood how deep their love was. I am so proud to be able to share their story.

Writing this story was a labor of love for me and I enjoyed every minute. I exercised my rights of artistic license for certain parts of their story that would have been weird and uncomfortable to talk about. I am sure the reader will figure it out.

I consider myself a very lucky man to have grown up in the family I did. I thank my lucky stars every day.

Mom, I kept my promise; I am a man of my word.

Kate's Diary,

Dear Diary,

I have to start you because I usually talk things out with Sunny but I can't. I can't because of stupid Jack Johnson. If he was in front of me right now, I would punch him in his face. He is an asshole and I hate that word, but I just can't help it.

I cannot remember life before Sunny. My earliest memories include Sunny. Even though we are not related or live in the same house, we are sisters. I know blood sisters that are not as close as Sunny and I. Or so I thought.

That is the hardest part for me to cope with. The fact that she didn't confide in me or ask for my help. I would take a bullet for her, but she did it all alone. How could she? More importantly, why would she? I knew something was wrong, I never thought this. I know that I told her that we will get through it together part of me is really pissed off at her and the other part is furious with Jack. He should have known. What an asshole.

When I saw her tonight with that bottle of pills in her hand I was really scared. Her eyes were dead, like she no longer cared whether she lived or died. I went into full protection mode. After I took the bottle from her hand, I searched around for anything else she could use to harm herself. Sunny is always so full of life and now she's just not present. I think I even hate Jack a little bit. I am not sure how I can help her heal. I know I can't stay mad at her so I may as well try and figure out how to help. First, I think she may need a little space to work some stuff out. I'll give her that, but not too long.

Sunny is hardly coming to school at all and if she does, she doesn't go to class. I noticed she is starting to hang around with the pot heads. I tried to include her into some normal activities. I wanted her to come with me to pick up our prom dresses. That's when she informed me, she won't be going. I kind of understand but I also think it will be good for her to come. Selfishly, I can't even imagine being at prom without her. Every major life event we have experienced together.

I remember the first day of kindergarten like it was yesterday. We had the same dress but in different colors. Our moms shopped together and let us pick out our first day outfit. My dress was pale yellow with a belt of daisies across the front. I had little white lacey anklet socks and shiny black shoes. Sunny's dress was lavender. Everything else was exactly the same including our hair. Big banana curls cascading down our backs with the cutest daisy barrette at the top of our heads. The day is immortalized by an eight by ten photograph hanging on our wall.

We stood at the bus stop waiting nervously for the big yellow bus to take us away from our homes and each other. I can remember feeling like I was going to throw up my Cheerios. Sunny spotted the bus coming up the block first. She took my hand, interlacing our fingers. "This is it, Kate, big school girl." I know she sensed my fear. We sat in the front seat together, never letting go.

She walked with me to my class first and went to hers across the hall. Later in the day, our classes passed each other in the hall. Sunny reached out and squeezed my hand. "Kate, isn't this the best? I love school!" Her joy was contagious. It eased my anxiety.

It's my turn. I need to grab her hand now.

I stopped in on my way home from school. When I stepped in, I could feel the tension in the house. Joann and Gary were just sitting silently in the living room. I kissed them both and ran upstairs. I didn't knock, just went right in. Sunny was just lying-in bed staring at the ceiling, tears in her eyes. I laid down next to her.

"I'm the worst person ever, Kate."

I rolled on my side to look at her. "You are not, you are just going through a bad time."

"I know I'm making my mom crazy, but I can't bear to tell her the truth." The tears started flowing more freely.

"Sun, you'll tell her when you're ready and I am always here for you."

She didn't say another word. I stayed by her side for over an hour and then I kissed her cheek and went home. Tomorrow is another day.

Finally, prom night was here. All of the plans and preparations we made were coming true. I couldn't enjoy any of it. I went through the motions and plastered a fake smile on my face. But I missed Sunny. It wasn't the same without her. I kind of felt bad for my date. He was a really nice person and I was excited to go with him. That was before, when Sunny and Jack were going too. Christopher was the perfect gentleman and took me home and walked me to the door. I never heard from him again.

I walked to the podium to get my diploma and didn't bother looking in the stands. I knew my sister wasn't there. I was proud of myself and really looking forward to my last summer before college, but there was that one little thing missing and I hate it. Now, she's not even going to work in Sprinkles this summer. She left for Kismet, without even saying goodbye. Hate him a little more.

I feel like she is pushing me away and I don't know what to do. The girl I work with at Sprinkles said she went to Kismet for dinner with her parents and she saw Sunny drunk at the bar. When she got up, she almost fell, and she didn't even recognize her when she said hello. I know I have to figure out a way to get through to her. I think I'll go visit her and see if she will come home for the weekend.

I stepped off the ferry in Kismet. The air was had that wonderful salty smell like the Fire Island I know and love. There are wagons at the ferry and kids willing to wheel your stuff to your house for a couple of dollars. It is still paradise for kids and adults alike. But it doesn't feel the same. It is very different from Ocean Beach. There's only one little store and two restaurants. My eyes drifted to one lone wagon that hung from its' lock.

I was rooted to the spot as a memory flooded my mind. A smile washed across my face. It was the summer Sunny and I were about nine or ten. We really wanted an ice cream cone but didn't want to ask for money. We wanted to make our own money. We collected shells and painted them. We tried selling them in town, but my dad is the only one who bought one. As we were walking back to the house, sad by our lack of success we saw the ferry arrive. We looked at each other and yelled, "WAGON!" We ran the rest of the way back. We grabbed the ferry schedule and the wagon. We stood there several times a day waiting for the passengers to make their way down the ramp with their bags and suitcases. We would yell, "wagon, wagon here." The rest of the summer we made enough money to keep us in ice cream cones every day.

I walked over to the Inn where Sunny works. My eyes scanned the room for my bestie. We spotted each other at the same time, and she looked happy to see me. Sunny came and gave me a big hug. "Hang out until I get off?"

"Yeah and let's go to the beach and gaze and talk."

"Let's go next door and drink first." Sunny started to wipe down the table. "Tequila makes the stars look better anyway."

"How about one shot and then we go to the beach?"

"Deal." Sunny kept her word. I worked at convincing her to come home. I tried my best to get her to open up. She started crying. She can't forgive herself for the abortion or keeping it from Jack. She's drowning her sorrows in alcohol and apparently now drugs too. Hate him some more. I was scrambling in my head to find the words to make her stop. If I could get her to come home just for a day, I think it will help. Joann and Gary will be thrilled too. I not even sure exactly what I said to convince her but I was so thankful when she finally agreed. We gazed up at the stars for a while and I longed for the easier times when we did this or those Sunday nights listening to Psychic Mike. *THAT'S IT! I need to get a reading with Psychic Mike!*

I brought Sunny home and ran in for a quick hug from Joann and Gary. Joann whispered thank you in my ear as we hugged. I just shrugged my shoulders not sure if it was going to make a difference. In the long run it actually did. She told her mom everything and that was a burden lifted off of her. I still can't believe Jack has never tried to call her. He really turned into a GIANT asshole.

After spending the day together, I took Sunny back to the ferry and noticed she wasn't as empty as she had been. I think I had a part in that, and it makes me feel proud. I was going on and on about college, I am so excited to start soon because I am going to be an amazing teacher! Soon my Sunshine will be back, and things can start to normalize. Also, I need to get that appointment with Psychic Mike. Wow, I have a lot to do!

I started making phone calls and asking around to get a private reading. This was more difficult than I thought. There was a waiting list to see him a year long. I was asking around during lunch one day at school and one of the girls I was sitting with said she had an *in*. I got two readings with the psychic and it cost me half of what I made at the ice cream store for the summer. I didn't mind because I think it will really be worth it. I think I will just leave out the part of how much it cost when I tell Sunny.

Sunny and I had a great lunch today. It reminded me of the old days, before the Jack attack. Still an asshole. I told her about our appointments with Mike. I picked Sunny up about thirty minutes early because I was so excited. I got my tape recorder ready and went in first. Mike was smaller than I imagined. He made me feel calm and welcome with little effort. We sat facing one another and he smiled. "Go ahead, ask me what you want." I was startled.

"Will I meet my soul mate?"

"Kate, you already have and I'm going to leave that with you."

I nodded in agreement wracking my brain as to who my soul mate is. He told me that I would help children as well as have many of my own. I asked him if Sunny would be okay and he assured she will be just fine and she will also reconnect with her soul mate. All I thought was, please don't tell me the asshole is coming back. Whatever, I am happy for me.

Sunny and I were in the car just looking at each other for a few minutes. Sunny spoke, "He knew about the abortion."

"WHAT? How the hell could he have known?"

"I don't know but he said that my baby is ok, and I am thankful. Thank you for this amazing gift, Kate. You are the best. I love you."

I believe Mike, we are going to be okay. I dedicated myself to my studies always keeping my eye open for Mr. Right. Sunny moved to the city and I am totally ok with it. I really miss her, but she needs to get herself together. She couldn't possibly go to school because of Jack, plus she didn't graduate, because of Jack. Yup, still an asshole and I hate him. I tried to get into the city about once a month to see Sunny. We would do touristy things together; it didn't matter what. It was nice to be together.

At the beginning of my third semester, in my evening class, I was running late and couldn't find a seat. I caught eyes with a really hot guy and kind of forgot why I was in the room. He motioned for me to come over and gave me his seat. It was warm and there was this fresh, clean scent that lingered. He smiled and my stomach started to flutter. Then he turned and walked out. What the hell? Why did he leave? The professor started speaking and I did my best to tune in. It was extremely difficult to get Mr. Hottie off my mind. I was thinking about going to find him when he returned with a chair. He whispered, "Mind if I share your desk?" I shook my head *no* and shifted in my seat.

At the end of class, he leaned in and introduced himself. "I'm Nate, thanks for sharing the desk with me."

"I'm Kate and it was my pleasure." He picked up his books and graced me with that amazing smile again.

"I know who you are," and he walked out.

I jumped up and dropped my books everywhere. I gathered my stuff and hightailed it into the hall. I looked both ways, but he was gone. How was I going to be able to wait two days to see him again? I really needed to see him again because I think I just fell in love. That man is hot, and I want to know him better. I couldn't even remember where or what my next class was. I should probably just go home. No, I can't do that. Think…where am I going? I started walking to my next class, the whole time just thinking of Nate. I didn't even notice him as I entered the classroom. He called out to me.

"Right here, Kate, I saved you a seat."

"How the heck do you know me?"

He started laughing. "I just met you five minutes ago."

"Yeah but you said you knew who I was." She wanted to touch his face.

"I'm insulted you don't know me; we have been in many of the same classes for the past couple of semesters. I wasn't sure what I should do to make you notice me."

"There's no way I didn't notice you." Kate wondered how this was even possible.

"I was in your freshmen seminar, freshman composition, child psych one and now child psych two. You always seem preoccupied, so I decided to make you notice me."

"Well, Nate, I'm glad you did. Let me make it up to you, come to lunch with me, my treat."

We sat in the school cafeteria and talked nonstop. I was enamored by him. I adored the way he placed his hand on my arm as he spoke. It made my knees quiver. I felt this unbelievable connection with him, and I really wanted to kiss him right there. When he let his smile loose it was like there were ten thousand butterflies in my stomach. When he asked me out on a proper date for Saturday there was no way I would say no. I would go into the city next weekend, I needed to go out with Nate like I needed to breath.

Nate picked me up Saturday afternoon. The cloudless sky was cerulean blue and the temperature perfect. He took me to the Bayard Cutting Arboretum. At first, I thought it was a strange place for a date. But he knew so much about the history of the place. Nate knew all about the evergreens and plants. My whole life I passed the entrance here and never gave it a second thought. I see it in a different light now, through Nate's eyes and it's magnificent. Nate took my hand and we walked around for hours talking and examining the fauna. He would point out a plant to and tell me the scientific name and all the facts about it. I know it sounds boring but to me, it was dazzling.

We walked over to the bay and sat for a bit. I felt like we were the only people in the world. My mind was racing. In those few quiet moments, I saw a happy life we could have together, the whole package. I was brought back to earth with a soft touch to my face and Nate leaning in for a kiss. In that moment, my fate was sealed. He was my one and only.

I couldn't wait for him to meet Sunny and I couldn't wait for her to meet him. The next weekend I went into the city and told Sunny all about him. I felt that my old friend was really back, and I hope it was for good! Yup, still think Jack is an asshole.

I can't believe how much I love going to college. I love every assignment, paper, class and even just walking around campus. Especially on Nate's arm now, it just made it even better. I can't wait until I have my own class! I am hoping to teach second grade. They are so adorable, and they are little people with their own personality. I think that would be the perfect grade to teach. I hope Sunny meets someone as wonderful as my Nate.

Sunny is on her way over, she's out this weekend having dinner with her parents and she has something exciting to tell me. I can't wait, I wonder what it is.

Well, her exciting news is that she is back together with Mr. Asshole Face. She says they talked it all out and everything is great, but I think I am going to wait until he proves himself to me. No way am I buying this crap. Let's just wait and see. Trying not to believe he is still an asshole.

I can't believe Nate and I have been together for more than a year. I have been wracking my brain to try and come up with the perfect Christmas present for him, but I did it and I am going to give it to him after the Marino's Christmas Eve party. I was so excited I forgot I was going to see Jerk; oops I mean Jack. When I walked in, he was the first person I locked eyes with. He smiled at me with kind and loving eyes. Eww. Jerk. Sunny was looking at him with such love. He held her to his side and my resolve started to melt. Nate felt me stiffen at his side. He asked me what was wrong. I looked at him and told him I needed a minute to talk with Jack. Nate knew everything of course and he kissed me on the cheek and said remember, it's Christmas.

I tugged Jack's arm and motioned with my head to follow me. Which he did, dutifully. I let him have it. I told him how he nearly destroyed my friend and abandoned her. I let him know how angry I am that he left her the way he did and that he if hurt her again I would track him down and hurt him worse. The jerk smiled. He put his arms around me and kissed my forehead. He held me by my shoulders, looked directly into my eyes and promised me that he regretted everything that happened and that he loved Sunny with every fiber of his being. Ok, not an asshole anymore. I hugged him back and he whispered how glad he is that Sunny has me. I started smiling too. I told him that I am part of the package and we were friends too.

Of course, Nate made our engagement plans for my maximum happiness, he knew I would want Sunny right there and he and Jack discussed it that night! How did he even know I would forgive Jack? I guess he knew I would. I can't wait to marry him. Start our happily ever after. I want a New Year's wedding. Yes! The planning begins tomorrow.

OMG, Jack just called, and he is going to ask Sunny to marry him. Not on her birthday, he wants her to be super surprised. I am so happy for them and I am starting to love Jack too! He has a grand plan and needs our help! I just want to jump up and down.

Went off without a hitch! Now we're all getting hitched. Hahahaha.

They are getting married in two months! She's crazy, how is she going to get everything done?

She did it! Best wedding ever! Until mine and Nate's. which is just around the corner. OH MY.

Well, the day is finally here. My wedding day. Yes, I'm getting married today. Holy moly. Diary if I don't write in you for a while it's because I'll be busy being a newlywed.

Dear Diary,

It's been many years. Too many. I forgot all about you. I remember writing down my thoughts, good or bad and how it made me feel. It always made me feel better. So why not try again, I could use it today.

I have had a wonderful life so far. I have four ridiculously handsome sons and one still amazing husband. I guess I was so busy being a newlywed I never picked you up again. Sorry. Sunny and I stayed close as sisters always. We raised our children like siblings too. I don't think we could have done it any other way if we tried. Ray is such a wonderful man and he is my fifth son. He and my Michael are inseparable. All of the boys are close but those two are just like me and Sunny. Thank goodness. Ray is going to need Michael to lean on now. I still can't believe it. Jack is gone. He just didn't wake up this morning. As soon as Sunny called I called Michael to go pick up Ray, so he didn't have to drive. We arrived at the house before the coroner and I am glad we did. They didn't need to do that alone. We stood around him in silence and then one by one said goodbye to Jack Johnson. The world just lost one of the best men it had. There was a knock at the door, a tall man in a dark suit entered and spoke with a gentleness in his voice which was completely soothing. It was time for them to take him. We all went into the sunroom, arms around one another we stood barely breathing. In this moment things would never be the same and we weren't ready to acknowledge it. The man with the kind voice came in. He let us know that they were done and leaving. We walked behind the stretcher, me holding Sunny and Michael holding Ray.

So tonight, as I looked through old pictures and memories, I found you. Maybe Jack wanted to remind me of our amazing history and how we are forever bound to each other.

His star is smiling down on us.

Thank you, Jack, I love you.

Dear Reader:

I compiled a playlist of songs from Sunny and Jack's story. I hope you enjoy listening as much as I enjoyed creating!

You're My Best Friend by Queen
Walk This Way by Aerosmith
Juke Box Hero by Foreigner
Dancing in the Moonlight by King Harvest
Baby I Love Your Way by Peter Frampton
Miss You by The Rolling Stones
Unforgettable by Natalie and Nat King Cole
Kiss on my List by Hall and Oates
Baby Hold on to Me by Eddie Money
Bad Case of Loving You by Robert Palmer
Ain't no Sunshine by Bill Withers
Sexual Healing by Marvin Gaye
What a Wonderful World by Louie Armstrong
Walking on Sunshine by Katrina and the Waves
Addicted to Love by Robert Palmer
Another One Bites the Dust by Queen
Foreplay/Longtime by Boston
Fool in the Rain by Led Zepplin
Paradise by the Dashboard Lights by Meatloaf

Love of My Life by Queen

Heaven by Bryan Adams

Have I Told You Lately by Rod Stewart

Greatest Love of All by Whitney Houston

Brown Eyed Girl by Van Morrison

Emotional Rescue by The Rolling Stones

Beast of Burden by The Rolling Stones

Start Me Up by The Rolling Stones

Only Wanna Be With You by Hootie and the Blowfish

Everything I Do I Do For You by Bryan Adams

Thinking Out Loud by Ed Sheeran

I Lived by One Republic

Heavenly Day by Patty Griffin

A Sky Full of Stars by Coldplay

Stars by Grace Potter

A little bit about me…

It took me a long time to figure out what I wanted to be when I grew up. I pursued my education later in life and earned a BA in Cultural Studies and MS in Childhood Education, all the while raising a family and working. I have had many different jobs and believe they paved the way to unleash the writer inside. I found joy.

I am a lifelong resident of Long Island. I have been married to the same man for well over thirty years. We have two handsome sons, Arthur and Justin. We are lucky to live a wonderful life.

Thank you!

Sometimes a simple thank you does not feel adequate. This is one of those times for me. I am grateful to everyone who took the time to read my book. I am appreciative that you became part of my journey to introduce Sunny and Jack to the world.

I also want to thank all the people who participated in my journey to bring Sunny and Jack's story to life. From the bottom of my heart, I appreciate all of your help. I am not going to list everyone's name, you know who you are, especially my Beach Wednesday group. I love all of you.

Connected by the stars, divided by one choice.

Sunny and Jack meet one night under the stars, and they are captivated by each other. Before long, they realize that they are destined to be together. Sunny and Jack are inseparable until distance tears them apart. In spite of that, they find a way to stay connected.

Sunny and Jack make a date each week to listen to music under the stars. It gives them comfort to know they are doing the same thing at the same time. The song in their hearts grows with each day, and their love deepens.

Sunny finds herself facing a difficult decision and she has a choice to make. She believes in her heart that the choice she'll make is the right one. But will that one choice tear them apart? Can the stars that brought them together keep them united? Will Sunny and Jack's love survive?

ISBN 978-1-6475039-5-6

www.austinmacauley.com/us

US$13.95 / C$17.95
£9.99 / AUS$21.95 / NZ$22.95

Austin Macauley Publishers™
LONDON · CAMBRIDGE · NEW YORK · SHARJAH